Safe in his Arms at Christmas

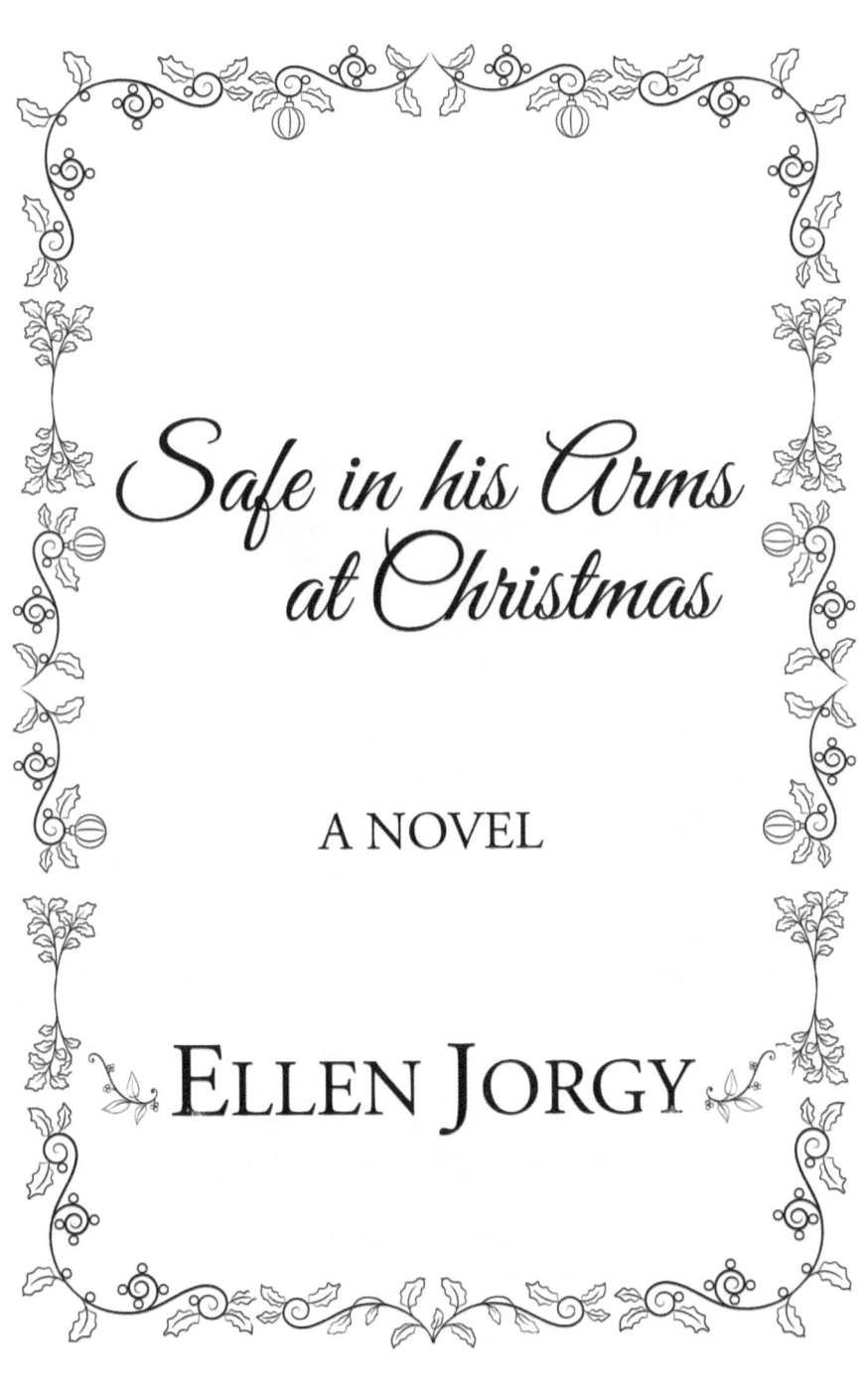

Safe in his Arms at Christmas

A NOVEL

ELLEN JORGY

Published 2021 by Ellen Jorgensen

ISBN: 978-0-9953035-4-6 (Digital edition)
ISBN: 978-0-9953035 -5-3 (Print edition)

Design and cover art by Su Kopil, Earthly Charms
Copyediting by Ted Williams

DEDICATION

To Bob.
Always safe in his arms.

ACKNOWLEDGMENTS

Thank you to my beta readers, Katie O'Connor, Victoria Chatham, and Karen Jorgensen. Your advice and comments were much appreciated. You ladies are amazing.

Thank you to Constable Jeff Erb of the R.C.M.P. for his insight and feedback on my police related scenes. Thank you, Jeff, for all you do to make the world a better place. "The authorities are God's servants, sent for your good." Rom 13:4

Thank you to Pastor Jachin Mullen from Home Church, Red Deer, for allowing his most wonderful church to be used fictitiously in this novel.

A special thank you to the very talented Su Kopil from Earthy Charms Designs for crafting another beautiful cover for me. I absolutely adore it. Please check out her website at www.earthlycharms.com to view her designs.

Thank you to Ted Williams for your precise and detailed line editing. An excellent job done well, as usual.

Thank you all my fellow authors who collaborated on the anthology "Hugs, Kisses and Mistletoe Wishes" of which my novel, "Safe in his Arms at Christmas", was a part. To Roxy Boroughs, S. L. Dickson, Raine Hughes, Shelley Kassian, Katie O'Connor, Sherile Reilly, and A. M. Westerling, thank you for inviting me to join in this fantastic Christmas project.

Finally, thank you to my husband, Bob, who patiently waits while I write away into all hours of the night. I love you, Bob.

CHAPTER ONE

*N*icole Mitro huddled in the warmth of her idling car, staring up the laneway while fear and hope battled for supremacy within her soul. The little white farmhouse with its red trim certainly looked nice. There was a fenced pasture in front, and big windows offered a good view of the lane, so no one could sneak up to the house unseen. Hopefully, the other sides had big windows, too. She didn't want to be blindsided again.

A half dozen large goats in the snowy pasture eyed her suspiciously from behind a woven wire fence. One bleated loudly. That could be helpful, too. An early warning system that didn't depend on electricity.

Okay. This just might work. Of course, anything would be better than being back in the city - back with those people - whoever they were. At least here she wouldn't be looking at everyone, wondering, 'was it you?'

Nicole put her little Honda Civic in gear and drove up the lane to park on the east side of the house. Footprints in the snow led to a covered porch. She slipped out of her car, slamming the door as the wind whipped her hair across her face, and followed the tracks to the door. She hesitated a moment, then forced herself to knock.

Short and slightly plump, with light brown hair showing gray roots, the lady who opened the door wore navy wool slacks and a red scoop neck sweater that brought out the flush on her cheeks. Her smile was wide and warm, but her blue eyes seemed a bit puffy, as if she'd been crying.

"Hello. You must be Nicole. I'm Corrie. Come on in." She stepped back, opening the door wide.

"Hi," Nicole offered shyly. She hesitated, peering past Corrie to the room beyond. Were they alone? Heart racing, she wiped her sweaty palms on her jeans. How ridiculous was she, to be so scared of an old lady? Nicole straightened her spine, forced a smile, and stepped into the house.

"Kick your boots off here in the mud room, and there's a peg on the wall for your coat," Corrie instructed. "The laundry room's through the door, on the right, and the kitchen is just beyond."

Nicole followed along, noting all the windows and their line of sight outside.

"You can see the big house where I live through the kitchen window. It's just a short way farther up the drive." She gestured vaguely up the lane.

Nicole turned to her left and moved through the door to the living room. Sun poured through a big, south-facing window. She could see all the way down the lane to the road. Almost perfect. There were some poplar trees lining the roadway that would bush out come spring, but maybe they could be pruned back so she could see the road better.

"It's nice," Nicole said. "Nice and warm on such a cold day."

"It may be an older house, but it's well-built and well-insulated. My husband, Abram, built it over forty years ago." Corrie's voice wavered, and she quickly turned her back to Nicole. She cleared her throat. "Anyway, there's three bedrooms and a bath upstairs."

Corrie led the way upstairs. The bathroom was at the top, and there was a bedroom in each of the other corners connected by a central hallway with a railing by the stairwell. The master bedroom wasn't much larger than the other two, but it had a big closet and south view towards the road. She'd be able to see anyone coming up the laneway. Her terrified heart calmed a bit. She could feel safe here.

They went back downstairs, her step a little lighter than before. "I love it. It will be perfect, I think. About the rent… You said it was negotiable in your ad?"

Corrie smiled, looking a bit worried. "Is it just you renting, Hon? All by yourself? No…husband? This is a three bedroom, after all. I was expecting a family or a couple at least."

"Yes. Just me. Is that a problem?"

"Well… Maybe not. I was going to ask fifteen hundred dollars per month."

Nicole felt her heart drop. Fifteen hundred? That might have been okay before she went off work on stress leave, but now her budget had been drastically cut. This place was perfect, the best one she'd seen. Nothing else had been even close and she'd already given notice at her old place. She needed something by December first. She swallowed hard.

This was so much safer than her old basement suite. It was quiet, out of the way, with no junkies down the street. No noisy neighbors snooping in the window. Nicole clasped her hands together tightly.

Corrie's expression softened. "However... I was going to offer reduced rent in exchange for some help around the farm. Maybe eight hundred dollars? My husband hasn't been well, and he recently took a turn for the worse."

"I can do that," Nicole said in a rush.

Corrie blushed. "Are you sure, Hon? You're not exactly built like a brick you-know-what. You're such a little, bitty thing. Do you think you're up to hauling water buckets and hay bales around? The small bales are a good seventy pounds, some of them, and I thought there'd be a man around to do the heavy stuff."

Nicole tried to look convincing. "Oh, Corrie, don't you worry. I used to visit my grandmother's farm when she was still alive. I've hauled a bale or two in my time. It will be fun to help out with the animals."

Hauled a bale of straw to sit on near the fire pit, maybe. But really? How hard can it be? "What all needs doing?" she asked.

"Well... there are chickens that need to be fed and watered, and their coop needs to be shoveled out and cleaned when it starts to stink. The goats need hay every morning and their water topped up every evening, plus some grain and alfalfa to fill their bellies overnight. Things aren't too busy this time of year, but come spring I'll need some help in the garden of course."

"Of course." Goats? Oh boy. Those things out in the pasture had horns. Big ones.

Nicole stood to her full five foot two and glanced in the mirror on the wall. A pale, heart-shaped face framed by shoulder-length, straight, dark hair stared back at her. Her light gray eyes were rimmed with charcoal around the iris and echoed the contrast of skin to hair. A startling face, some had called it. Dramatic, elfin, with well-defined cheekbones and gracefully curved brows. All she could see was the shadow of a bruise still marring her cheek. She'd haul water and feed goats in a blizzard if it meant not having to live in the city again.

"I love it already," she offered. "I don't mind helping out wherever you need me. When can I move in?"

Dr. Garrett Pine examined the little, dark-haired girl carefully, looking in her ears and down her throat. Her lungs sounded good, as did her heart. She was a little underweight, but otherwise healthy. He swabbed her skinny arm with alcohol and gently pinched the skin while inserting the needle. A second later, the vaccination was complete with barely a whimper from the child.

"All done." He smiled at her as she clung to her mother. She did not return his smile, but regarded him with large, solemn, brown eyes. She looked exactly like an owl.

The child's mother was definitely smiling back at him

though. He'd seen that smile all too often, a little too bright, full of hopes and dreams. Dreams about to be dashed. Dreams he had no intention of fulfilling.

Garrett cleared his throat and stood up, feeling awkward. He came down to Mexico every fall with 'Doctors Without Borders' to offer his services and help the poorest of villages, not to find a young Mexican wife, no matter how pretty she might be.

A wife was something he couldn't indulge in right now. He just wasn't reliable enough to manage a career and a family.

"Doctor Pine. There's a call for you in the office." One of his fellow volunteers called through the open door.

"Perdón," he said to the young mother, grateful for the excuse to leave. Her disappointment followed him out into the hallway.

Who could be calling on the Sat phone? "Hello?"

"Garrett? It's Mom."

"What's wrong?" Garrets stomach twisted. He remembered the last time she'd called unexpectedly. His old guilt rushed back in, flooding him with shame.

"It's your Dad, Garrett. He's had a stroke. It's pretty bad. I know you're busy, but…can you come home? Please? He wants to see you."

"Of course, Mom. You know I will. I mean, I'll try. I'm out here in the middle of nowhere, so it will take a bit longer… But I'll make it happen." He'd messed up before, but this time he'd get home as fast as he could, before it was too late.

"I know you will, son. I can always count on you."

Garrett hung up the phone and sat in the cramped little room that subbed for an office, staring out the dusty window. She actually sounded like she meant it. Yet, where had he been ten years ago? Not there on the farm where they needed him. Not helping out his dad like he should have been. Farms are dangerous places and he'd let them down. No more of that. He'd help them now. He'd get them off that farm and into the city where they'd be safe and closer to the hospital.

CHAPTER TWO

*N*icole sat in the middle of her new living room surrounded by boxes and discarded packing paper. The sun shone brilliantly through the window, doubly bright for having bounced off the snow outside. Even with the frigid weather, the little farmhouse was warm and cozy. She couldn't help but smile. It was so much safer here.

Her closest friends had come through for her, helping pack and move her on short notice, although that meant the boxes had been packed haphazardly with nothing labelled. But beggars can't be choosers as they say. She was just happy to be out of her old place.

A knock at the back door made her jump. She got up, heart pounding, and peered out the living-room window. Of course, the back door was set inside a covered porch and she couldn't see who was there. She padded quickly through the kitchen to the mud room and approached the door carefully. She peeked out through the small window in the door.

A sigh of relief whooshed out. It was just her new

landlady, Corrie. She unlocked the door and opened it to a gust of icy wind.

"Hi. Come on in." She smiled a welcome for the older lady. She *really* needed a deadbolt. That little doorknob lock wasn't good enough. Why hadn't she noticed that before?

"Hello, Hon. Just thought I'd wander over and see how you were getting on." Corrie shrugged out of her parka and winter boots, hanging the coat on a peg on the wall. "I brought banana bread, if you'd like some."

"Mmm. That smells delicious," Nicole replied. She led the way back into the kitchen. "I'm afraid I haven't got much unpacked, yet, but I can probably offer you a cup of tea. I think I know which box has the tea bags in it."

"Oh, don't fuss over me." Corrie laughed. "I don't need anything."

She sat down at the table and surveyed the mess of boxes and paper. "Still have lots of unpacking to do, I see. Just put all the paper in a large garbage bag. I'll show you where to put it when you're done. We have a bin we put our recycling in until we can take it to the transfer station.

"I must say, I was quite surprised to have you move in so quickly," she continued.

"I was anxious to get settled as soon as possible. I hope that's not a problem," Nicole replied. She poured water into the kettle and plugged it in, then rummaged around in an open box looking for the tea.

"Not at all," Corrie said. "It's actually good for me. With my husband not well, I could use a little help around here."

"About that," Nicole said. "I must confess, I haven't much experience with goats. They look a little scary."

Corrie laughed out loud. "Oh, the girls won't hurt you, unless you get between them and their evening grain. Then they might run you over trying to get at it.

"They do love a good scratch on the back, however. On the whole they're pretty gentle. Now our buck is harder to handle, but I'll show you a few tricks to get around him. I'm sure you'll do just fine."

"I won't let you down, Corrie."

"That's good, Hon. Glad to hear it…Well, I'm off to the hospital to visit Abram. I'll show you around and fill you in on feed details when I get back, if that's all right?"

"Sure. That would be fine."

After waving goodbye to Corrie, Nicole carefully locked the door and tugged on it to make sure it was latched. She returned to the living room and stood, surveying the boxes. Her old winter coat, ski pants and extra gloves and hats were in there somewhere. She'd have to dig them out before Corrie got back. She didn't want goat hair all over her good winter coat and it was way too cold out to wear just a hoodie.

All her Christmas decorations were in there somewhere, too. She smiled to herself thinking about it. Christmas was only five weeks away. She could hardly wait. It was her favorite time of the year. She'd normally drive down to Arizona to spend it with her parents, but this year she'd stay in her new home. Corrie needed her help, and if she wanted to stay here, she'd best make herself useful.

It was too early to put up a tree, but if she could find her lights somewhere in the mess, she could put the outside stringers up this week.

With renewed enthusiasm, Nicole ripped open a box.

Books. Those would go on the bookshelf in the corner of the living room by the east window. She carried the heavy box over and started unloading the books onto the shelf. She shoved the last book into its place and started to flatten the empty box when she noticed a loose key in the bottom.

She picked it up and examined it, turning it slowly in the light from the window. What the heck was that for? It wasn't the key to the stairway door in her old basement suite. She'd given that back to Mr. Fellows when he'd gotten home and she had returned his cat, Norman, to him.

Norm. She sighed. She missed Norm. He was a good kitty. She used to sneak the stairway door open and let him come down for a visit and a cuddle on the couch. Maybe she would get a cat, if Corrie didn't mind.

Without a further thought she put the key up on top of the bookcase and started in on another box. She'd too much unpacking to do to worry about a random key.

CHAPTER THREE

*G*arrett pulled his Mercedes SUV carefully up to the little house and parked in his usual space. He sat for a moment with the engine idling trying to drum up the energy to move. He could barely keep his eyes open and his limbs felt leaden.

First he'd endured a five-hour drive on pock-ridden backroads to the airport in Mexico, then a three-hour wait to board the plane. A guy couldn't sleep in the airport for fear someone would stash something illegal in his carry-on bag. Then the flight to Calgary seemed to take forever. He'd gotten some sleep on the plane but not enough what with food service, crying babies, and filling out customs declarations.

He'd almost driven to his own place after claiming his SUV from long term parking, but home was at the far south end of Calgary, and his parents' farm was north of the airport by an hour. It was a bit farther to go to the farm than to go home but if he went home, there was no food in the fridge, and the coffee, if there was any, was probably stale. He still had some clothes stashed at the farm for emergencies, so he decided to drive straight there instead.

As he neared the farm, he realized it was almost midnight. Mom would have been asleep hours ago. He was dead tired but didn't want to wake her. He pulled up by the little house, his usual place to stay on the rare occasions he stayed over. There was a small car parked there, with a good inch of snow crusted on top. It obviously hadn't moved in a while and he was too tired to wonder about it further. Inside, nothing would be ready, but he knew where the spare blankets were stored, and a quick turn of the dial would get the baseboard heaters going. He'd have a warm place to sleep and could surprise his mom for breakfast.

Garrett turned off his engine and forced himself to move. He crawled out of the car, grabbed his carry-on from the back seat, and trudged through the cold to the back porch door. He lifted the mat to retrieve the spare key, then stood, dumbly shivering in the cold, staring at the bare floorboards. Where was the stupid key?

He looked around on the ground, moved the pot of dirt that would hold flowers come spring, checked the top of the door ledge. Nothing. Where'd she hide it?

Frustrated, Garrett decided he'd spent enough time shivering in the cold. The door had a little trick. He put his bag down and stepped up to the door. If memory served, all he had to do was turn the knob just so, apply a little lift up, and hit the door with his shoulder... With a thump and a bump, Garrett stumbled into the mud room. Back at last.

HUDDLING in the bedroom closet with the door closed and the phone clutched in her hand, palms wet with sweat, Nicole dialed the numbers frantically.

"Nine one one. What is your emergency?"

"Someone's breaking into my house!" she whispered in a hoarse voice. Her heart was racing and her breathing came in ragged gasps as adrenaline surged through her body. She was shaking so badly she could barely hold the phone. Another bump and thud downstairs made her jump.

"What is your address, please?"

Nicole panicked. "I don't know. I don't know! I just moved in this week. Somewhere east of Innisfail, in Red Deer County. Please hurry! I'm all alone here," she whimpered.

"We're tracing your phone. I have officers on route."

"How long until they get here?" She could feel her blood surge, and time slowed down. Each heartbeat thumped painfully in her ears. Every sound from outside the closet was magnified.

"I can't say for sure, Miss. They're on route. Please stay on the line."

Nicole hadn't realized you could yell and whisper at the same time until that moment. "They're inside my house! I hear someone on the stairs."

How could this be happening? Her safe place? Broken into all over again. Mind-numbing panic surged through her. It was happening all over. She needed help now. She couldn't wait, not a moment more.

"Please stay on the line. Keep talking. I need to know what's happening to update the officers."

I can't wait. I need help now! Nicole hung up and pushed

the number for Corrie. At least she was right next door. *Oh God, help me!*

GARRET HUNG his jacket on a peg in the mud room and flipped on the kitchen light. He wandered through to the living room too tired to pay attention to his surroundings. He bent over to turn on the baseboard heater before realizing it was already warm.

Huh. Mom must have turned the heat on early to be ready for him. He straightened, turned and cracked his shin on a coffee table that hadn't been there before. Wincing, he glanced around the room. She'd bought some new furniture, too. Lord only knew why. There hadn't been anything wrong with the old stuff, aside from being old, that was.

Garrett grabbed his bag and trudged up the stairs. Every step made that old familiar creaking sound. It was funny how things which used to drive you crazy as a teenager, now just seemed warm and familiar. This was home to him, not his parents' new, larger house up the lane. He opened the door to his old bedroom and then stood there, staring around blearily. His mom had left a bunch of boxes all over the place. What was she doing?

He turned around and went to his parents' former room before they'd moved into their new house a hundred yards up the hill from this old one. He opened the bedroom door and dumped his bag on the floor. At least this room was free of boxes, but it looked as though his mom hadn't cleaned up after the last visitor was here. Then he remembered his dad was still in the hospital. Mom likely hadn't had time for anything but Dad since the stroke.

A wave of guilt washed over him. He should have been here. But how was he to know? This farm was so much work. He should have convinced them to sell this place and move into town ages ago. That's something he could do, and he would, just as soon as possible.

He glanced at the bed. He was far too exhausted to go to the bother of changing sheets. He grabbed the blankets and pulled them up. Since the room was already warm, he'd just grab a quilt from the closet and wrap up in that tonight.

Garrett opened the closet door, and just about fell back at the ten-alarm shriek that assaulted his ears.

"Get away from me!" a woman screamed. "I have a gun!"

"Whoa!" Garrett threw his arms up, backing away quickly, all trace of drowsiness vanished. "Okay. Calm down. I'm not going to hurt you. I didn't know anyone was here," he said, trying to sound as calm and reasonable as possible.

"G-G-Get out of here. Now! The c-c-cops are coming." The female voice wavered from within the depths of the closet.

"Okay. Calm down. I didn't mean to scare you. This is my parents' house. I've just arrived home. I was going to sleep here so I didn't wake anyone up...but I'll go."

Garrett was backed up into the corner on the other side of the bed from the door. The voice in the closet sounded terrified, and the one thing scared people did was make stupid, rash decisions. He didn't want to be on the receiving end of any panicked blunder on her part. He eyed the doorway. Crawl over the bed or risk coming closer to the closet door by walking around?

He edged closer to the door.

"Stay back!" she yelled. "Go away!"

"I would love to accommodate you, sweetheart, but I can't do both at the same time. You've got me backed into a corner here. Literally."

He thought he heard a soft rustle from within the closet, then an eye peeked briefly through the crack of the door where the hinges were. Garrett held his breath.

Suddenly, there was a loud crash from downstairs as a door banged open.

"Any trespassers in here better GIT! I'm a-coming up the stairs and I've got a shotgun." Corrie's voice bellowed from below.

"Mom!" Garrett yelled. "It's just me. Tell this crazy lady to put her gun down."

There was a moment of silence, then, "Garrett?"

He heard the incredulous joy in her voice. The guilt washed over him again. He'd been away too long.

"Garrett!" Corrie barreled into the room, dumped the gun on the bed, and wrapped her arms around his waist in a bear hug.

"Careful, Mom, you don't want that thing to go off." He chuckled, surprised and happy to be welcomed so warmly. He glanced at the closet door, hoping the crazy lady wouldn't come out shooting.

"Oh, don't worry. It can't. It's not loaded," she answered, releasing her grip on him. Her face was flushed and she was grinning ear to ear.

"Mom." Garrett stepped past her to the 12-gauge on the bed. "It's still got the lock on. You can't fire it like this."

"Well, of course not. Someone might get hurt. Besides, your dad's the one who knows where the key is."

"What are you doing waving around a useless, locked gun?"

"Well, the bad guys wouldn't know it was locked. I was just trying to scare them away." Corrie stood back, hands on hips, as if this were no big deal.

"Anyone with half an eye can see the cable lock, Mom. For heaven's sake, are you trying to get yourself killed?" Garrett sighed loudly and ran his hand through his hair. She had a death wish. He was way too tired for this.

"No, I was not. I was *trying* to rescue Nicole... Oh! Nicole, honey. Are you okay?"

Corrie bustled over to the closet. Garrett stepped back and watched, intrigued, as his mother bent over and drew up the sweetest, tiniest young woman he'd ever seen. Wrapped in blue checked pajamas, she couldn't be more than a hundred pounds, one ten at the most. He stared, unable to look away.

Even with tear stains on her cheeks, she was exquisite. Her dark, chocolate brown hair was disheveled around her pale cheeks. Her rose-pink lips formed a perfect cupid's bow. But her eyes, a light clear gray rimmed with charcoal, bore into his soul. They still looked haunted, terrified. She was shaking all over. Guilt stabbed him.

His mother wrapped her arms around the young woman and held her tight.

Nicole took a huge, shuddering breath. "I - I'm okay." She buried her face in his mother's shoulder.

Nicole's eyes flicked his way and pink stained her cheeks. "What were you thinking?"

"I was thinking I was home and I wanted to get some sleep. But I'm sorry. It's my fault. I should have called... Or knocked. I shouldn't have assumed..." *Stop babbling like an idiot, Garrett.* "Why didn't you just say something instead of hiding in the closet?"

The look of death she hurled at him shut him up. Maybe she had a point. He'd obviously terrified her. Garrett cleared his throat, and shoved his hands deep into his pockets.

"Do you normally break into other people's houses?" If looks could kill he'd have withered on the spot.

"I didn't realize someone was living here." Garrett's temper flared. "I normally stay in my parents' guest house when I visit."

Her icy gray eyes just glared at him over the edge of his mother's shoulder. They reminded him of a predator, when they'd noticed something to chase down and kill. "You called me crazy," she accused. "You break into *my* house, and then you call *me* crazy."

"Look. I've already said I'm sorry. Okay? What else do you want?" Garrett glared right back at her. How was he supposed to know? It's not like anyone kept him in the loop.

"Well, this is awkward," Corrie stated, glancing back at Garrett. Nicole still clung to Corrie, while the older woman patted her back.

"Nicole, this is my eldest son, Dr. Garrett Pine. Garrett, this is my new tenant and farm help, Nicole Mitro."

CHAPTER FOUR

*N*icole forced herself to step back from Corrie's reassuring embrace. She was still trembling but the terror was starting to recede, and embarrassment was taking its place. How humiliating. Hiding in a closet while freaking out was a great way to meet her landlady's son for the first time. She wiped her sweaty palms off on her pajama bottoms before accepting the handshake he offered.

His hand was firm and warm in her chilled grasp, but the expression of his cobalt-blue eyes was cool under the barely there beard he sprouted.

"Hello," she said, feeling foolish about hiding in the closet.

"Farm help?" Garrett's question was directed towards Corrie, although his gaze still locked with hers. It made her feel uncomfortable, like she was being dissected.

"That's right. Farm help," his mother said. "With your dad in hospital, I'm spending a lot of time there. I've offered Nicole reduced rent in return for helping out with the chickens and goats. Your brother's taken over the cattle operation, but he's too busy with that to deal with the smaller livestock."

"Goats?" He dropped her hand and turned to face Corrie. "*Goats?*"

Nicole could see the displeasure on Garrett's face. His tan, and the gold highlights in his caramel-colored hair, suggested he was recently home from a tropical vacation, but the dark shadows under his eyes suggested exhaustion rather than relaxation. He wasn't impressed, that was for sure.

What was wrong with goats? They were pretty cute from what she'd seen earlier that day when Corrie had shown her around the barn and pens. A little pushy when it came to their grain, perhaps, but rather adorable on the whole.

Almost on cue, one of the goats let out a loud 'maaa' and was echoed by a few others.

"What has the girls upset, I wonder." Corrie went to the window and peered out. "Oh, my! What on earth?"

"What is going on?" Garrett asked, going to the window to peer out. "There's a.. no. Wait. There are *three* police cars in the yard. There's a cop looking in the front window downstairs."

Oh no! How could she forget?

"I, I called the cops... When I thought you were an intruder," Nicole confessed.

"What did you tell them? That there was a mass terrorist attack going on?"

"No. I just told them I heard someone breaking in. And then I hung up to call Corrie."

"You hung up?" Garrett's voice rose a notch. "Didn't you say it was okay when they called back?"

"They called back?" Nicole felt stunned, she hadn't noticed. She looked at the notifications on her phone. They had called. Repeatedly.

"They always call back. Why didn't you answer?" Garrett demanded.

"I didn't hear it. I turned the ringer off so it wouldn't give away my hiding spot."

"They think you've been killed!"

Nicole's face flushed. "Well, I was scared. You broke into my house."

Garrett rubbed his palm on his face. "Okay, okay... Mom, stash the shotgun under the bed. You're not supposed to be waving that around even if it's not loaded. We'd better go downstairs and meet them at the door. They'll want to make sure you're all right, Ms. Mitro."

SOMEONE POUNDED on the front door. "POLICE."

Corrie opened the bedroom window and called out, "We're okay. Everything is fine. We're coming down now."

Nicole grabbed her fluffy pink housecoat and, feeling like a complete idiot, wrapped it around herself as they filed down the stairs.

Nicole opened the front door with Garrett and Corrie standing just behind her to find three stern-looking officers waiting. They wore blue parkas and matching blue body armor overtop with the word 'POLICE' across the front.

"We received a dropped 911 call. Is everything all right here? Is there a Nicole Mitro here?" The first officer, whose name tag read as 'Wilson', was tall, dark-haired, and serious looking.

There were two other officers standing just behind him, an older man with salt and pepper hair, and a blond woman, perhaps thirty, both wearing blue police toques, and both with weapons drawn. They all looked tense, like they were ready to pounce at the slightest wrong move.

"That's me," Nicole said, raising her hand tentatively. "Everything is fine, now. I - It was just a misunderstanding."

The palpable tension in the air eased off slightly as the two officers re-holstered their pistols. Nicole let her breath out in a whoosh, only now aware she'd been holding it.

"Do you mind if we come in and talk?" It was more a statement than a question. "Ms. Mitro, is there a place to speak in private?"

"Yes. Of course." She opened the door farther and led Officer Wilson towards the kitchen.

Out of the corner of her eye she saw Corrie being drawn aside by the female officer in the living room, and Garrett being led out onto the porch with the other officer.

"So what happened here tonight?" Wilson asked after closing the kitchen door.

"It's all so stupid. I'm sorry I called you for nothing," Nicole said, feeling her face flush. "I really thought it was a home invasion. I just moved in here, and I guess the landlady, that's Corrie in the other room there, didn't tell her son, Garrett, that I had moved in. He let himself in tonight, thinking the place was empty. And I freaked out. I had a real break-in last month in my old place in Calgary, so I'm kinda jumpy I guess..." she trailed off, feeling foolish as Wilson wrote down some notes.

After a few more questions and reassurances that she was under no duress and everything was fine, Officer Wilson said, "Wait here, please."

He left the kitchen to confer with his fellow officers. A few minutes later he re-opened the kitchen door. Nicole went with him back into the living room where Corrie and Garrett now waited on the couch.

"All right then," Wilson said, sounding far more relaxed than he had when he'd first arrived. "Your stories all match, so it seems we do just have a misunderstanding here. Officer Delaney is just doing a quick check of the house to make sure you're not being threatened by someone else hidden here but otherwise we'll write this off as a mistake."

Delaney came back down the stairs moments later. "All clear," she said, smiling.

"Again, I'm really sorry. I didn't mean to cause a scene," Nicole apologized.

"That's all right. As long as it's not deliberate mischief, we don't mind. You folks have a better evening," Wilson said cheerfully. "Oh, and Ms. Mitro? Don't ever feel that you can't call us if you feel threatened, especially after the incident in Calgary. We don't mind coming out to check on you even if it turns out to be nothing. Better safe than sorry. Have a good night."

"Th-thank you," Nicole stammered. She could feel eyes penetrating the back of her head as she watched the officers climb back into their cars and drive off. Great. Now she'd have to dodge questions about Calgary. She wasn't ready to explain that to anyone.

In the pasture by her house, luminous goat eyes reflected back at her out of the dark. "Maaaa," one of them said.

'Ma' indeed. What a night.

CHAPTER FIVE

"*R*eally, Mom? Goats?" Garrett sat at his mother's kitchen table in the southeast corner of her house nursing a cup of coffee.

He'd been home a couple of days now, catching up on sleep and reconnecting with his mother. His one visit to his father had been dismal. Dealing with his father's illness wasn't an issue. He did that all the time as a doctor. It was dealing with his *father* that was the issue. They had looked at each other, but he hadn't known what to say, and his dad was unable to speak. It had been awkward and painful, and something he was in no rush to repeat.

Things needed to change. That was obvious. He was more determined now than before but wasn't quite sure how to make it happen.

From his spot at the table he could see the barn and Nicole, bundled up in a parka and pair of inadequate city boots, trudging along the snow-packed path from her house towards the chicken coop. He took another sip of coffee, his belly full of home-raised eggs and fried bacon. He didn't remember things tasting so good before. Mom's cooking really was the best.

"Well... I needed some brush cleared out down in the gully. It was breeding mosquitoes like crazy in the spring. Made sitting on the porch very unpleasant," Corrie replied as she tidied up after breakfast.

"They have chemicals for that, Mom. Goats are expensive and a lot of work."

"So are chemicals." Corrie sat down beside him with her own coffee. "I don't want to spray a bunch of toxic chemicals all over my land. Besides, I'd still have to go in there after everything died and clean out all the dead sticks and branches. This way, I just let the goats go in there and they eat everything down to the ground, even small trees. They're very efficient. They even fertilize as they go." Corrie chuckled and winked at him.

"Do you really want to be out in the cold, at 30 below, feeding goats all winter?" He could see it now. She'd slip and fall in the snow, break her hip, and be frozen solid before anyone found her.

"I don't have to." His mom looked smug. "That's what Nicole's for."

Garrett scowled. "I highly doubt that girl has a clue what she's doing. Did you see those boots she's wearing?"

"Give her a chance, Garrett. She just moved in last week. The goats seem to like her at any rate."

Garrett shook his head, took another swallow of coffee. It sat like a rock in his belly. This was as good a time as any to broach the subject.

"You know, Mom. You could just sell. You'd get a lot for this place even at auction..." From the look on her face, he knew he should shut up, but he plowed on anyway. "I know you don't want to hear this, but this place is a ton of work and Dad may not make it..."

"Just you stop right there." Corrie stood abruptly and marched to the counter where she shoved her empty cup. "Your father is going to be fine. Fine! Do you hear? And I'm not selling. How would your father feel? When he gets out of the hospital and finds out I sold the farm out from under him? I won't do that!"

"*If* he gets out, Mom..."

"*When* he gets out. And not another word from *you,* Mr. Smart Doctor. Now, I'm going to the hospital to see him. Are you coming?"

"I'll go a little later," Garrett mumbled. "One guest at a time, I think."

"Fine."

Corrie grabbed her coat from the back of her chair and, without a backwards glance, left through the kitchen door. He watched her cross the wrap-around deck and go down the few steps to her waiting car. She didn't even bother to warm it up before backing up and driving away down the lane to the township road. He watched the cloud of snow crystals follow her car, until it had disappeared down the road.

Well played, Garrett. Way to handle that. Some things never changed, apparently.

He let his gaze drift over towards the little house directly south of him. What was that crazy lady up to now?

"Oh, for Pete's sake!" Garrett leapt to his feet, grabbed his coat off the peg by the door, shoved his feet into his boots, and flew out the door.

Perched on the top of the ladder, Nicole fumbled with the clips to hold her Christmas lights onto the gutter along the edge of the roof. Her cold fingers were stiff and awkward in their gloves. She dropped another clip but managed to get the next onto the gutter. She grabbed the dangling string of lights and leaned over, trying to get them onto the clip as well. Ugh. The wire was so stiff. She leaned out a little farther, trying to adjust her grip.

The ladder shifted. She let out a shrill yelp as it teetered. She clutched the gutter, arms straining as she tried to reverse her tilt, and then her ladder suddenly stabilized.

"Are you trying to kill yourself?" The voice of Dr. Garrett Pine accosted her.

Nicole looked down to find him scowling up at her, gripping the aluminum ladder in his bare hands, wavy brown hair blowing in the frigid wind. His ears were bright pink. From cold or anger, it was hard to tell.

"Not on purpose." She scowled back, fingers clamped onto the gutter like vice grips. "I'm trying to put up my Christmas lights."

"Get down off that ladder before you fall," he demanded.

"What about the lights, Mr. Bossy? Or should I say *Dr. Bossy?"*

"Just come down." He glared up at her. "We'll put them along the fence line. You can't see your own lights if they're up on the roof. Out along the fence, you can see them from your front window. That's what we always did when I was a kid."

Nicole swallowed, took a moment to calm her racing pulse, let the fright recede slowly, like water draining from a clogged sink. She inhaled deeply, let the air slide back out to vanish in a puff of white on the wind.

She looked out, across the yard. She had her own fenced area south of the house down to the road. There was another fenced area between her little house and the big ranch style house north of her. Behind her, there was a fence running along the east side of the lane from the road up towards the barn. She imagined how they would look covered in lights. Hmm. Maybe Dr. Bossy was onto something.

"We can do *all* the fences. They'll look great from the road, too!" she exclaimed.

"*All* of them?" Garrett didn't sound thrilled.

"Of course," Nicole said. "Your mom doesn't have time to decorate. It will cheer her up to come home and see the lights. We can put them up around her porch too. It will be beautiful."

"Fine. Fine. Just get down here. This ladder is freezing my hands off."

Nicole climbed down slowly. What a grump. Maybe all that education had drained the fun out of him.

As she neared the bottom, he released the ladder and stepped back to make room for her, but he placed his hands on either side of her hips, steadying her descent. Nicole's heartbeat jumped a notch. His hands were ice cold, but they still made her thighs glow with heat. She reached the ground and turned to face him, finding her nose level with the open button of his shirt. She had to kink her neck to meet his blue, blue eyes. He watched her intently. His breath came out in a gentle plume of steam.

Nicole took a step back, cleared her throat. "Um, thanks for rescuing me up there."

"No problem. I owed you one after scaring you the other night." He shoved his hands deep into his pockets, stepping back farther yet.

"Yes. Yes, you did." Nicole's cheeks went hot, despite the weather. She wanted to be mad at him, blame him for her crazy overreaction, but now that she'd calmed down, she could see his side of things a little better. "But I guess I did overreact a little," she admitted.

"Don't worry about it. It was my bad. If you're determined to put up lights, we'd best get at it. I need to go back up to the big house and get my hat and gloves, and some long johns. Are those the only boots you have?"

Nicole looked down at her feet clad in black leather calf-high boots with a one-inch heel. "Yes. They're winter boots. I'll be fine."

"If you say so." Garrett didn't look convinced. "Go inside where it's warm until I get back. It may take awhile to dig out my mother's Christmas lights, if I can find them. I know where they used to be, as long as she hasn't moved them."

Nicole watched his back as he strode up the lane towards Corrie's house. Even with his shoulders hunched to keep his ears below his collar, his stride was long and easy. His shoulders were broad and his waist lean. That, right there, was a very sexy man. She sighed, watching him retreat. There was a time she might have pursued him, but not right now. How could she? How could she trust anyone, especially someone she'd only known a few days?

It was odd. He seemed to dislike her, but then he ran out to save her from falling, and now he was helping her with Christmas lights. So many mixed signals from him.

She went back into her house to take off her boots and warm her chilled toes by the radiator while she waited for her grumpy neighbor to return. Her toes stung with cold already. She probably needed better boots but that could wait until later this week. Decorating came first.

Her need to decorate was at compulsion level after nearly being scared to death. She had to make this place look beautiful. She needed lights, decorations, wreaths and more. Her new home had to look so amazing, so wonderful, that it would drown out the memory of what had happened at her old place. When she looked out the window, she wanted to see a Christmas fairytale, not a nightmare.

a couple of hours later, the Christmas light installation was well underway. Nicole's fence line was finished, as was Corrie's, and they were almost finished the section along the driveway to the barn. Looping the stringers over the fenceposts in a scalloped fashion was much faster than trying to attach them to the roofline way up in the air. The only things remaining were the wrap around porch of the big house, and the spruce tree in Nicole's front yard.

In spite of all the walking, Nicole's toes were complaining of the cold. She'd tried wiggling them, and stomping her feet, but the minus fifteen celsius was seeping in and her feet felt like blocks of wood. Her fingers were stiff with cold, too. Good thing they were almost done.

She glanced longingly at her warm little house, but clamped her mouth shut. If she said anything, he'd want to stop, and maybe even help her warm up. She couldn't allow that. The other night had been terrifying. Even though she knew now it was all a foolish mistake, she couldn't let him back into her house. It just didn't feel safe. Even the thought of it had her throat tightening in fear.

"Why are you walking like that?" His question came out of nowhere.

"Walking like what?"

"You're walking funny, like you can't feel your feet." Garrett strode through the snow towards her, little puffs of ice crystals floating up like clouds with every step. "Your feet are frozen, aren't they? Those stupid city boots may be fine for getting from your car into the house, but they're just not warm enough for farm chores."

"I'm fine. They're just a little cold. We're almost done anyway." Nicole winced as she took a step toward the rest of the lights.

"Can you still feel your toes?" Garrett asked, taking the stringer from her hands.

Nicole turned away, looking down the lane, away from him. What could she say that wasn't a lie? Her silence seemed to tell him everything he needed to know.

"Okay. We're done for today. Let's get you inside to look at those toes." He tossed the remaining lights back into the box by the fence.

"Look at? What do you mean 'look at'?" Panic wrapped its tentacles around her chest and squeezed tight. "I said I'm fine. I'll be fine. You don't need to look at anything." Her voice rose higher with each statement.

"I don't believe you. Inside. Now."

Nicole couldn't move. She stood there, staring at him, trying to focus her eyes, as the tentacles tightened further. It was hard to breathe. She started shaking. Everything was moving too fast, but she was sinking in quicksand, unable to move. Her pounding heart drowned out everything else. She tried to move but her brain was as frozen as her toes.

"Nicole?" Garrett's worried voice drifted to her dimly.

She took one step, stumbled, and he was there, catching her.

"Come on, sweetheart. You need to get inside. Don't be afraid." His voice was calm, smooth as butter, almost a caress. He scooped her up in his arms as if she were a feather and carried her towards her home.

"I... I'm not afraid," she stammered. A tear eased down her cheek, as she clung to his neck, unable to stand and fearful of falling.

"Of course not," he said gently. "You're going to be fine." His arms tightened around her a fraction.

Garrett carried her all the way into her kitchen and eased her onto one of the hard wooden chairs. Slowly time resumed its normal speed, and Nicole found herself shivering uncontrollably. He disappeared into the living room and came back with a throw blanket from the back of her couch. He wrapped it around her shoulders and tucked it over her thighs.

"Are you okay?" He crouched in front of her, looking up into her face, little lines of worry etched around his eyes. Kind eyes. Eyes that maybe saw too much.

Nicole nodded dumbly. She couldn't trust her voice. What had come over her? He was a doctor for heaven's sake. He was just trying to help and she... she must be having a panic attack.

"Let's have a look at those feet." He slowly eased her boots off, one at a time, then her socks. "They feel like ice," he said with no censure in his voice. He pressed gently on her great toe. It looked pale and waxy. "There's no capillary refill. You have first degree frostbite already. Any longer outside and you may have lost a toe." He stood up, went over to her kitchen cupboards and started rummaging through them.

Guessing what he was after, Nicole said, "Bowls are far right, bottom."

"Thanks." He found a large one and started filling it with water.

He brought the full bowl over and guided her feet into the water.

"Ow," she cried. "It's hot!" Her feet felt like they were on fire. She tried to pull them out, but his hand stopped her.

"It's not hot. It's barely lukewarm. It only feels hot because your feet are so cold."

Nicole huddled in her blanket, feet burning up in tepid water. It all seemed too much. Calgary, the other night's terror, now frostbite. Having this kind man trying to care for her and feeling afraid of him. Her eyes began to brim over. A tear splashed down onto the blanket.

He noticed, crouched in front of her. "Hey. It'll be okay." He reached up towards her face.

Nicole flinched back. She didn't want to. She couldn't help it. She glanced at him. Would he be angry at her for that involuntary action? Her heart fluttered like a bird trapped in a cage, desperately trying to escape.

"Hey," he said softly. "What's wrong? You're not afraid of me, are you?"

"I - I'm sorry." She took a deep shuddering breath and dropped her gaze down to her feet. "I know it's silly but..."

"I'm not going to hurt you. I would never hurt you. Please believe me."

She looked up. He was still crouched there, in front of her chair. Close, but not touching her. Being there, but not intruding. She met his eyes. He looked concerned, sad even, but not angry. Why had she thought he'd be angry? She felt some of the tension slide off her, and allowed herself a timid smile.

He smiled back. It lit his face, like the sun rising over the ocean. Her smile cracked a bit wider.

"Has this got anything to do with what that police officer said to you the other day? What happened in Calgary? Did you have a break-in?"

Nicole bit her lip and looked away. Should she tell him? She barely knew him. He was so complicated. On the one hand he seemed so grumpy and bossy. On the other...she looked back at him. Crouched here in front of her, he seemed to care deeply. Deep blue eyes, like a stormy sea, watched her every expression. She glanced away. What would he think? That she was an idiot? That she deserved what she got for being so stupid and naive?

"Why are you here? With me? Helping a near stranger put up her Christmas lights instead of visiting your father in the hospital?" *Dodge and deflect, girl. Dodge and deflect.*

Garrett's open expression shuttered like an old house before a storm. He stood and moved towards the cupboards again. "It's complicated."

"Try me," Nicole pressed.

"You need something warm to drink. Coffee or tea?" he asked.

It's supposed to be coffee, tea, or *me,* she thought, but only said, "Tea."

"Tea it is. Um… where?"

"Middle cupboard, center."

Garrett made tea as Nicole wiggled her toes in the water. Their color was gradually returning, and they were tingling like crazy. He placed her cup on the table beside her and took a seat on the opposite side with his own cup.

"Thank you," she murmured.

He nodded and took a sip.

"You're not dodging my question that easily." She stared him down across the small table.

Garrett shrugged. "Dad's not really with it right now."

"What's wrong with him?" Nicole sipped her tea, starting to relax more now that the conversation wasn't about her. Feeling the fright dissipate into the room, leaving a gentle warmth in its place.

"He had a stroke. Mom says he has good days and bad. He can't speak, and he can't swallow, so he'll be in hospital until he can eat on his own."

"You should go see him. Even if he can't speak, he'll know you're there."

Garrett scowled down into his mug. "It's not that simple. I couldn't talk to him when he was well. I have no idea what to say now that he's not."

"You and your dad didn't get along?"

"Not really. I was always a disappointment to him."

"That can't be true. I mean, you're a doctor, aren't you?"

"I suppose. I'm just in general practice though."

Nicole couldn't believe her ears. She chuckled to herself. "*Just* a doctor. *How* disappointing."

"Well, I guess it is if you're looking for help around the farm and your kid won't get his nose out of a book long enough to be useful." Garrett stood abruptly and turned away, sliding his mug onto the counter behind the table. "I'm just here to support my mom," he mumbled, looking out her window toward the big house.

He came back around to crouch in front of her. "Let's see how your feet are doing."

Nicole withdrew one foot from the water, extending it towards his waiting palm. The warmth of his hands surprised her, sending a wave of heat up her legs and beyond, causing her face to flush. He looked up abruptly, almost as if he'd felt it, too, and his eyes met hers. Nicole's breath caught in her throat. Wow, he was handsome. And kind, and smart... how could he ever feel like a disappointment? He had to be wrong. Surely Corrie and her husband couldn't be disappointed in Garrett as a son.

He stared at her a moment, then seemed to force his attention back to her feet. "The blood's starting to come back to your toes." He checked her other foot. "Yes. Much better."

"Thank you. They're starting to feel almost normal."

He grabbed a kitchen towel and handed it to her, then stood back, hands jammed into his pockets. "I think you'll be fine, but you need to keep your feet warm today. No more outside chores for you. We can finish the lights in a few days, after I take you to get some decent boots."

"But I still have to feed the goats and chickens," Nicole protested.

"I'll do it. You just keep your feet warm. Maybe go have a hot bath." His face reddened, then he cleared his throat, turned around, and headed towards the mud room.

"Do you know what to do?"

"I grew up here, remember?" He shoved his arms into his coat sleeves. "I'll figure it out."

Nicole stared at the door he'd disappeared through. It felt like something vital had just vanished, like the air she needed to breathe, or the rays of the sun. Whatever was going on in her head?

CHAPTER SEVEN

*W*eren't goats supposed to be cute? Small, cute, bouncy bundles of energy and fun?

The face that was staring him down could hardly be described as cute. Malevolent might be a better word. Malevolent, determined, and powerful. A plume of steam shot from its nostrils in the frigid air, and Garrett could easily imagine it as dragon's smoke.

Topping up the chicken feeders and water had been easy. Even feeding the female goats, the does, hadn't been too bad, although there'd been a lot of pushing and shoving as they all tried to get the grain in his bucket before he was ready to pour it out into their feed pans. This big guy was something else, though.

Fenced separately from the girls, in the yard between the two houses, the huge brown and white buck stood planted in his pen, between the gate and the feed dish. He had a head like a concrete block, with a flat face that flowed into two massive horns making his head look like a giant claw hammer. He was at least two hundred pounds of bone, sinew, and muscle. Definitely not 'cute'.

"Hey, buddy. Ready for supper?" Garrett spoke calmly to the beast.

The buck raised his head, glaring down its long Roman nose towards Garrett. Was this why Satan was often drawn with goat horns? Okay. Here goes.

Garrett opened the gate and slipped into the pen, closing the gate behind him. Keeping an eye on the buck, he walked slowly around him on the well packed snow towards the feed dish. The buck didn't rush at him, but with the slow confidence of a champion heavyweight boxer walking through a gang of five-year-olds, the buck came forward, easily pushing Garrett aside to access his grain even as it was poured out.

Garrett stood beside him for a moment, watching him eat. He sunk his fingers into the goat's plush winter coat and gave him a little scratch on the back while the animal was distracted by his supper. The white fur was almost as thick as a sheep's and had that same oily texture that would protect him from snow and rain. He also smelled pungently of goat, unlike the does who were penned on the other side of Nicole's house. Garrett wrinkled his nose.

Scratching absently, Garrett let his thoughts return to Nicole. Had he really suggested she have a bath? And then imagined her naked in a tub surrounded by bubbles? He groaned inwardly. What was wrong with him? The last thing he needed was to get involved with some farm-loving crazy person.

If he wanted to get his parents off this farm and into a nice condo in town, she was going to be a problem. Why on earth was she out here anyway? He should probably have let her fall off the ladder. If she broke an ankle, she wouldn't be able to help on the farm, and it would be that much easier to get his folks to sell.

Garrett shook his head. What was he thinking? He could no more stand by and watch someone get hurt than he could stop his heart beating. And standing by was something he'd vowed never to do again, not after what happened with his father.

Garrett's heart softened, thinking about Nicole. Those striking grey eyes of hers had just about stopped his heart back in the kitchen when she'd pinned him with her gaze. It still hurt to think she'd been afraid of him. Despite her protests to the contrary, she had been. He was sure of it. He just couldn't figure out what he'd done to cause her panic attack. It must have something to do with whatever had happened back in Calgary. But what?

Beside him, the buck raised his head, and eyed Garrett with one evil rectangular pupil. Uh oh. The beast had finished his grain. The goat pushed its shoulder into Garrett's thigh in an unspoken challenge. Garrett stepped back and began walking back towards the gate. The buck followed closely, almost touching his leg. At the gate, Garrett had no room to open it.

"Back off there, buddy," Garrett said, placing his hand on the animal's head. He pushed firmly, trying to move the goat aside. It was like trying to push aside a car.

The goat dropped his head lower, stamped a foot, and hummed a low threat deep in his throat. The beast still blocked the gate. Garrett took a step back, recalculating. Maybe he could climb out?

"Nor-bee. Here you go, Norby." Corrie sung out in the musical voice she reserved for use on her creatures. She stood just outside the pen swishing the contents of an old margarine tub, likely a handful of grain, back and forth.

"Garrett, get out of that pen when Norbert comes over this way."

At the sound Norbert raised his head slowly, glared at Garrett, then turned and sauntered off towards the food. Garrett slipped quickly out of the pen, locking the gate behind him. Thank God for moms!

"What on earth were you doing in Norby's pen? He isn't safe, especially if he doesn't know you."

"I was feeding him," Garrett replied. Why did he feel like a five-year-old caught with a box of cookies under his bed?

"Where's Nicole? This is supposed to be her job."

"She is recovering from frostbite. I told you those stupid boots of hers were no good."

"Oh dear. The poor girl. We'll need to get her some better boots. The farm store will have lots still. It's early in the season. They may even have some Christmas specials on."

Garrett started walking back up to the main house, side by side with his mother. He wanted to say 'Let's just sell this place', but the words stuck in his throat. There'd be time for that later. For now, she seemed to have forgotten the morning's argument, and Garrett simply wanted to enjoy being her son for a while.

He glanced back over his shoulder to where Norbert stood in his paddock, glaring between the fence boards, watching them. Garrett chuckled at the goat's expression, and called out, "Yeah, yeah buddy. I know. You still reign as the supreme being around here."

The goat raised his chin and huffed out a puff of steam as if to say 'and don't you forget it'.

CHAPTER EIGHT

*N*icole sat beside Garrett in the passenger seat of the Ford F250. Her new waterproof neoprene muck boots, warm to minus forty, sat in their box in the back seat. When she'd balked at the price, Garrett had insisted on paying for them. He'd seemed cheerful about it then, but his mood had soured the closer they got to the farm auction mart.

Garrett turned into the auction yard and parked the big truck with its trailer alongside other similarly parked units.

"Put your new boots on. No telling how many animal sales we'll have to sit through before they get to the hay. Why Mom waited until she was completely out baffles me," Garrett grumbled.

"My feet will be fine," Nicole answered, adding, "I'm sure she's been busy with your dad. I should have told her sooner."

"Yes, you probably should have." Garrett's blunt response rebuked her. What on earth was eating at him? So they needed more hay. So what?

Trailing behind, she followed Garrett across the yard and into the building. Thankfully it was heated, and though not exactly warm, she was in no danger of losing a toe in her old boots. Garrett registered for the sale, which was already going strong in the next room. On impulse, Nicole registered her credit card, too, and got her own auction card so she could bid.

"What do you need that for?" Garrett scowled at her.

"I might want to buy something." Nicole lifted her nose and stared him down. Funny how she could be brave everywhere but her own home.

"What are you going to buy? A cow? Gonna keep it in the pantry?"

"Ha ha. Very funny. I don't know. Maybe I won't buy anything. I've never been to one of these."

Garrett shook his head but led the way into the next room. Tiered raised benches encircled a dirt floored round pen where a half dozen cattle were currently on display. The auctioneer rattled off numbers and comments so quickly they seemed to blur into one long incomprehensible word. They climbed up to the top row and sat down where they could lean back against the wall.

"Sold!" The gavel came down with a bang and the cattle were ushered out one door to be replaced immediately by another bunch coming in from the opposite side of the ring. Some were large and fat and went for high prices, often whole herds being sold in a batch. Other cows were small and sickly, selling cheap in twos and threes to people who seemed to be willing to take a chance on fattening them up.

Nicole watched it all, fascinated. Beside her, Garrett

leaned back in his seat, chin on his chest and an old cowboy hat pulled low over his eyes. She wasn't sure if he was just resting, bored, or actually asleep.

It took awhile, but when the cattle were finally done, smaller animals were brought in. Nicole watched a few batches of goats and sheep sold before a single, sad-looking, white and brown goat was ushered into the ring. Her belly was huge, but her hips stuck out from a bony back. She had lopsided horns, her ears drooped, and her head hung low.

"What's wrong with her?" Nicole poked Garrett in the ribs.

Garrett grunted softly, pushed his hat back and sat up to look. "Looks like she's underweight and likely pregnant. Could have some disease I suppose, but most likely they just weren't feeding her enough. She'll go cheap for meat." He leaned back again, arms folded across his chest.

"Pregnant? *Meat?*" Nicole leaned forward, eyes focused on the poor doe in the ring. It raised its head and looked right at her. Nicole's heart melted.

"I have thirty, thirty, thirty. Do I hear thirty-five, thirty-five, thirty-five?" The auctioneer's voice rattled off numbers like rounds from an automatic rifle. "Going, going, going?"

Nicole's arm shot up with her card.

"I have thirty-five, thirty-five, thirty-five. Do I hear forty, forty, forty?"

"What are you doing?" Garrett demanded in a stage whisper, glaring at her from under the brim of his hat.

"I'm saving her. Poor momma goat."

"Forty, forty, forty?"

"What are you going to do with her? She'll need to be

quarantined in case she does have a disease. You can't put her in with the others."

"Going, going, going,"

"I'll figure it out."

"No. You can't buy a goat."

"SOLD!" The gavel slammed down.

"Too late now. She's mine." A satisfying surge of triumph emboldened her.

Nicole met Garrett's glare straight on. A smug smile tugged at the corners of her mouth. Garrett's frown deepened. *Too bad for you, Dr. Bossy.*

"I guess I'm a goat owner now." She grinned.

"You're crazy." Garrett turned back to the ring and ignored her until he'd successfully bid on some hay in small square bales.

ALL THE WAY home Garrett had barely spoken two words to her. She'd done nothing more than stand aside and watch as the auction employees had thrown hay bales onto the trailer floor while Garrett did the hard work of lifting and stacking them at the front of the long cattle hauler. He'd then pulled the truck and trailer up to the animal loading area to collect Nicole's new goat. He hadn't said anything, but his displeasure was obvious. After securing the goat in the back of the trailer he'd locked the door and climbed back into the truck.

Now they were almost home, and the tension was unbearable.

"I think I'll call her Mistletoe," Nicole said. Anything was better than this silence.

Garrett glared out the windshield.

"Did you hear me?" she persisted.

"What? Who?" Garrett glanced briefly at her before returning his attention to the road.

"My new goat. I'll name her Mistletoe because it's almost Christmas. Missy for short."

Garrett merely grunted.

"What is your problem?" Nicole asked. "You seemed fine this morning, but you've been miserable ever since we got to the auction."

Garrett spared her a brief scowl. "I just don't think you should be buying a goat."

"That's not it. Your mood soured long before I rescued Missy."

Garrett turned into their driveway, staring straight ahead. "All right then. I don't think Mom should have goats, either. I don't think we should be buying hay to feed them. I think we should be selling, not buying." He pulled the trailer up to the barn door and slammed it into park with a jolt.

"Why? What's wrong with goats? They're cute."

Garrett swiveled to face her in the front seat. "They're *farm* animals. They need to be on a *farm*. And I want to move my folks *off* this farm and into town."

Nicole's heart dropped like a stone in a pond. "Why?" Her voice sounded strange in her ears, whiney, like a petulant child.

"Because farm life isn't safe. It's hard, lonely, dangerous work even for someone who's still young and strong. My parents are in their sixties. They need to sell this place and move into town where life is easier and I can keep an eye on them." Garrett undid his seatbelt and slid out of the truck. "It's obvious my father is in poor health and Mom can't do everything by herself."

Nicole climbed down from her side. "But that's why I'm here. To help Corrie. How does she feel about this? She led me to believe I could stay here long term."

Garrett strode around to the back of the trailer and unlatched the door. "My mother is being difficult as usual. And you are definitely not helping."

"Excuse me?" Nicole straightened her spine and glared at Garrett. How dare he? "I do so help. I've done everything she's asked except a couple of nights ago when you offered to do my night chores."

Garrett stepped up into the trailer and unhitched Missy. He passed the rope down to Nicole. "Here's your goat. Take her into the barn and find an empty box stall to put her in. She'll need to be wormed and quarantined before we can put her with the other does."

Nicole snatched the rope and glared up at him. "I said, I do help."

"Not me, you don't. I want them to move, and you're in the way."

"Well, I wasn't brought in to help *you*. I'm here to help Corrie."

She tried to spin on her heel and march off with her goat. It looked so righteous and indignant in her mind, the two of them, storming off. The reality was less impressive. She took one stride and just about fell backwards when the goat planted her feet and refused to follow. What ensued was a tug of war where Nicole did all the tugging and the goat remained immobile, regarding her with a stubborn glare. Nicole made a final attempt, heaving with all her might, when her feet slipped out from underneath her, and she fell hard on her rump.

Garrett snorted.

"Very funny," Nicole snapped.

"Yes. It was." He grinned briefly, and the boyish good humor completely changed his appearance. The spark in his eyes set her heart alight. It was like the sun emerging from behind the clouds with all the warmth it could bring until his smile faded as abruptly as it had appeared, and the sun vanished with it.

He reached down and grabbed Missy by one horn. Lifting her front feet right off the ground with one hand, he force-marched her into the barn while Nicole climbed painfully back onto her feet.

Garrett strode back to where she stood. "So... You think you're farmhand material, do you?" He challenged.

"Bring it," she answered, jutting her chin out.

"Okay. Since you're determined."

His smile now looked more like that of the Grinch. Nicole felt apprehension trickle down her spine. What now?

Garrett swept his arm back to indicate the loaded trailer. "See all these bales? They need to be stacked in the far end of the barn, over there. They weigh roughly seventy pounds each, but there are only thirty of them. Have fun." His smile was evil as he turned around and walked away.

CHAPTER NINE

*N*icole got stiffly to her feet when the knock came at her back door. She already knew who it was, having watched Garrett walk down the lane from the big house towards hers through her kitchen window. She shuffled through the mud room to the door and cracked it open.

"Yes?" She stood blocking the opening, eyeing him suspiciously. Several days and several hot baths had done little to ease her sore aching muscles after unloading all those bales of hay. Her bruised butt cheek and bruised ego hadn't helped either. That, on top of seeing Garrett as a threat to her safe haven, had her feeling prickly as a cactus.

"I brought your mail." Garrett offered the small stack of envelopes to her.

"Thank you," she replied stiffly. Could he feel the ice in her words? She hoped so. She was just starting to love her new home in spite of this grumpy, bossy, maddeningly handsome man. She wasn't going to lose it without a fight.

She began to close the door when Garrett put his hand out,

stopping it just before it shut. "Look. About the other day…" he began.

"Don't worry about it," she interrupted. "You made yourself clear. You want them to sell, and I'm in your way." She raised her voice a notch. "But let me be clear. I want to stay. I'm finally feeling safe, and I'm not just going to go away for your convenience. If I have to join a gym and bulk up to throw bales twenty feet so I can stay here, then I will!"

"Yes. I see that now."

A gust of cold December wind forced itself past them into the house. Nicole shivered involuntarily.

"Can I just come in and talk a moment?" Garrett pressed.

Nicole hesitated. What was there to say? She saw the determination on his face and sighed. She pushed her misgivings aside and opened the door wider. "Fine. Come in."

GARRETT WATCHED, guilt poking him repeatedly, as she half hobbled back through the kitchen.

"Would you like a cup of coffee?" she asked.

"Let me get it. You look a little sore."

"You noticed," she said dryly. She shuffled to the table and lowered herself slowly to her chair.

Garrett turned away, feeling his face flush. "I'm sorry about that. I was trying to show you how tough it can be out here. I didn't really expect you to unload the whole trailer full. I figured you'd give up partway through, and I'd go out and finish it off for you. I wasn't counting on you being so stubborn." Or so beautiful. He filled the coffee maker with water and found the coffee and filters.

"Fooled you, didn't I?" she said.

He glanced over at her, and her eyes held him momentarily hostage. Their full dark lashes fanned briefly against her pale cheeks before lifting off like a bird in flight. He coughed and turned back towards the counter to break their hypnotic power. He'd come here to talk her into moving, not to become enchanted by her eyes, or the way her pretty pink tongue kept darting out to moisten her lips. The room was suddenly too warm for the light sweater he was wearing over his T-shirt.

He kept his back to her while he tried to focus on making the coffee and finding the cream and sugar. When it was done, he placed her cup beside her and moved to stand in the doorway to the living room. A bare Christmas tree stood forlornly in the corner of the living room surrounded by open boxes full of decorations.

"I see I've interrupted your decorating," he said, glancing back at her.

Nicole grimaced. "I tried to start last night, but I'm not moving too fast right now, and the high stuff was giving me grief." She sighed and stretched her shoulders slowly.

"I could help." Now why had he said that? Could it be he actually enjoyed the company of this crazy girl?

He saw the suspicion in her eyes as she said, "I thought you wanted me gone."

"Well… Not before Christmas, of course. And it's not like I want *you* gone. I'm just worried about my parents, and their safety. You can understand that, can't you?"

Nicole studied him from under her lashes. Safety she could understand, completely. But there was more than one way to be safe. Nicole could make things safe around here. She was here to help. She'd show Garrett that he was worrying over nothing. With her around, his parents would be completely safe from the dangers of farm life. Once he saw how well things were going, he'd relax and forget all about convincing Corrie to sell.

The alternative was dismal. Nicole thought about having to move somewhere without Corrie. She was always so warm and friendly, even with how worried she must feel over Abram. She was always popping over with baking or just to chat. It was nice to have someone watching over her.

"So… You want some help or not?" Garrett asked again.

Nicole turned her full gaze on him. What would it be like living somewhere without Garrett popping over to help her out unexpectedly? Her throat tightened thinking of it, which was strange. It wasn't like they knew each other well, or that they'd even known each other for long. Why should his presence matter? Somehow, it did.

"Sure. Why not?" She rose stiffly to her feet and slipped past him into the living room. His cologne enveloped her as she passed, a subtle mix of vanilla, musk and spice. She couldn't help breathing it in a little more deeply, savoring the scent that was all him.

He followed her into the room. She tried not to be too obvious as she watched him peel his sweater off and toss it onto the couch. The white T-shirt underneath stretched taut across a chiseled chest. Nicole averted her eyes and tried to focus on the decorations instead.

"How about some music?" Garrett asked. "Something to get us into the spirit of things."

"I have some Christmas CDs on the bookshelf. There's an old player here on the side table in the corner. Pick whatever you like."

An hour later the sad, bare tree sparkled like magic in a children's movie. Blue and purple lights entwined with silver tinsel garland encircled it round and round. Shiny baubles in matching hues scattered light across the branches in a never-ending dance as the lights twinkled on and off. Christmas carols played softly in the background, and the room smelled of the apple cinnamon candle Nicole had lit earlier.

"There are still boxes of ornaments we haven't even touched," Garrett said. "What do you mean we're done?"

"Yup. I have way too many to put them all on one tree. So I switch up my color scheme every year. Last year was red and gold. This year is blue, silver, and purple. Next year, who knows." She grinned.

Decorating the tree had been fun. Dr. Bossy had been anything but. He'd cheerfully done her bidding without argument or complaint, wrapping lights and hanging ornaments. Having a man-slave was something she could get used to. She secretly smirked to herself.

"The only thing that always stays the same is having an angel on the top, although I have one in silver, and one in gold, so they switch back and forth. Here. You can do the honors." She handed him a pretty angel, clothed in silver, with blond hair and ceramic candles in her hands.

Garrett took the angel with her tinsel-adorned gown and carefully perched her atop the tree. "What do you think?"

"That's perfect," she answered. And not just the tree either. Standing there, holding up the angel in his fitted jeans and tight T-shirt, he looked perfect, too. The tousled chestnut hair and barely there beard sent the sex appeal into overdrive. Nicole licked her lips. Delicious.

Garrett stepped back from the tree and surveyed the room. "It looks great in here. The pillows and other decorations. It's very artistic."

"Well, I hope so. I am an artist after all." Nicole chuckled, pleased that he liked the atmosphere she'd created.

"You are?" He sounded surprised.

"Didn't you know? I guess I never mentioned it. I teach college art in Calgary, or, I mean, I used to. I'm on leave right now." She felt her face flush and sat down on the couch to rest a moment before tidying up.

Garrett sat down beside her, so close he was almost touching her thigh. His cologne, divinely warm, washed over her and teased her senses alight. She inhaled deeply.

"Oh? Why's that?" He asked, sliding his arm along the back of the couch behind her. She stared at his mouth. His finely sculpted lips hovered on the edge of a smile. Her gaze darted up, caught on his, rested there. She licked her lips again, and watched his pupils dilate ever so slightly.

"S-Stress leave. I - I'm supposed to go back to work in January... But I don't think I'm ready yet."

"Calgary's a long commute from here. How's that going to work?" he murmured, never taking his eyes from her face.

"That's why I'm not ready. I'm thinking of Red Deer.

They have a college art program." She trailed off, her eyes still locked on his. His gaze dropped to her mouth, his Adam's apple bobbed. She leaned in closer...

Garrett stood suddenly, cleared his throat and ran a hand through his hair. The action tightened the T-shirt across his well-defined pecs.

Nicole sat back, tried to calm her racing heart, and swept the hair back off her face.

"I'd love to see some of your work one day," he said and stuffed his hands into his jeans.

"I have a studio set up, upstairs. There are a couple things I've been playing with, but nothing's finished," she offered.

"Do you mind if I see them?" Garrett asked.

"I guess not." She smiled, standing to her feet. "Follow me."

CHAPTER TEN

*G*arrett followed her up the stairs, trying not to stare at her cute little butt as she climbed. What was wrong with him? A short talk had turned into most of the afternoon helping her decorate and he still wasn't ready to leave. He should be telling her his plans, his hopes to move his parents into Calgary where he'd be closer and could keep an eye on them. But he knew how much she loved it here, and that she wouldn't be happy about having to move again herself.

At the top of the stairs, they turned right and went towards the sunny southeast bedroom that had been transformed into a studio. An easel was set up to catch the light, with a canvas showing a whimsical collection of goats, camouflaged by their patches of white and brown within the background of melting snow on dirt. He studied it with interest, enjoying how Nicole had created the feeling of intrigue. Were the goats really there, or was it just an illusion created by melting patches of snow and rocks? Garrett couldn't help but smile.

He recognized the face of Mistletoe with her lopsided horns amongst the others.

He turned to the other canvas, set up across the room beside a mirror on the wall and caught his breath. It wasn't finished but was obviously a self-portrait of Nicole. Her striking gray eyes, dark lashes, and equally dark hair were unmistakable. Half-drawn, half-painted, it was also two opposing halves of expression. Garrett moved closer.

"What have you done here?" he asked, awed.

Nicole blushed. "I'm trying to show two sides of myself at once. On the right, I thought very hard of a specific memory, and on the left I imagined things turning out very differently. Then I drew each side separately, meeting and blending them down the middle. I know. It looks weird. I'm not sure I like it."

"It's fantastic." He meant it, too. He leaned in closer. The image was a little disturbing, but not because of the juxtaposition of the two halves.

"Your expression on the right? What were you remembering? You look frightened."

Her blush deepened if that were possible.

"It's a long story. Maybe I'll tell you one day, but I still need to go feed the animals before it gets dark, and tidy up downstairs before starting supper."

His cue to leave. Fair enough. But he'd get it out of her eventually. Garrett offered his most charming smile.

"Lead on, then." He swept his arm towards the doorway and followed behind her down the stairs.

NICOLE PAUSED in the living room beside a box she needed to put away until after Christmas. Either she was a way better artist than she'd thought, or he was very astute. He'd read her face perfectly. Why had she let him see that? She wasn't ready to explain, maybe because the whole thing had been terrifying, and maybe because she felt that, somehow, it had been her own fault. Thankfully he hadn't pushed the subject.

She watched him put his sweater back on and start to leave until he paused by the kitchen door.

"There's still something missing," he announced.

"What's that?"

"Mistletoe."

"You think I should bring a goat in here?" she asked. "That would be kind of messy, don't you think?"

"No, crazy girl. Not the goat. The plant. You should hang it right here in the doorway between the kitchen and the living room." He walked to the spot and pointed up. "Right *here*."

She walked over to the doorway and looked up where he pointed at the bare archway, then at him. "And why is that?"

Garrett grinned. "So I can do this." He cupped her face in his palms, and dropped a brief, sweet kiss directly on her lips.

She gasped softly as a rush of warm pleasure swept over her. He straightened, looking almost as surprised as she felt. He took a quick step back.

"I should probably go." He strode through the kitchen and grabbed his coat off the peg in the mud room while Nicole stood rooted to the spot, stunned. He grabbed the door knob, paused, then turned back towards her.

"Oh, uh, Mom wanted me to invite you to join us for church tomorrow morning. We always go."

Still reeling, mentally, Nicole said," Um, sure. What time?"

"We'll pick you up at ten. Good night."

And he was gone.

Nicole stood immobilized where he'd kissed her. She reached a hand up tentatively and touched her lips where they still tingled. Did that really just happen? And how could such a full busy room feel so completely empty now that he'd gone?

GARRETT STRODE BRISKLY through the frigid air back towards his mother's house, snow crunching under his feet.

Now why had he done that? He'd just kissed her, like some kind of cave man. He was lucky she hadn't hauled off and smacked him for it. He hadn't even pretended to ask permission. Desire had spoken, and he'd just dived in. What was he thinking?

He needed to be more respectful of her wishes from now on, but he wasn't sorry he'd done it. The zing had surprised him, and what a nice surprise it was. Very nice, indeed.

Where was his good sense?

It was his own idea to invite Nicole to church, too. Now he'd have to come up with something to tell his mother to explain that. It was like his brain didn't work properly when Nicole was around. It must be her eyes. They melted his brain into jelly. Garrett shook his head.

In his pen beside the lane, Norbert bleated a loud complaint. He stood on his hind legs, front hooves propped up on the fence, and head leaning over the top rail. Garrett walked over to the fence to scratch his forehead. On his hind legs, Norbert could almost reach Garrett's chin.

"What's your problem, old man? Hungry?" Garrett scratched between his eyes. "Man, you're stinky."

Norbert hummed and reached out to nibble Garrett's coat sleeve. He grabbed a mouthful and yanked.

"Hey! Enough of that." Garrett pushed the goat back. "I'm sure Nicole will be out to give you your supper shortly." Too late, he realized pushing a male goat was a mistake.

Norbert stepped back, hummed in annoyance, then reared up on his hind legs and hurled his head and horns full force at the fence. He hit with a resonating smack that cracked one of the two by six boards along a weak spot. Garrett jumped back in surprise.

"Whoa! Dude. Calm down, buddy." He stepped back from the fence even farther. Mental note: Don't hit the goat.

Garrett continued his walk up towards the main house with Norbert following him up the other side of the fence line as far as it went, one evil eye glaring at him through the gaps in the fence boards. The gate to the pasture at that end was held closed by a piece of chain looped around the fencepost. Garrett made sure it was secure before going inside. He didn't want to find Norbert wandering loose, ever!

CHAPTER ELEVEN

"It's kind of odd, her asking to come to church with us, don't you think?" Corrie asked.

"I don't think so," Garrett said, keeping his eyes averted from his mother as he pulled up in front of Nicole's door. "She's new around here, and it's a great place to make new friends."

"I suppose so. Still, I should have invited her myself instead of waiting for her to ask. I've just been so consumed with your father's stroke. I really should apologize," Corrie continued.

"No. Don't do that. She might feel embarrassed if you do that. Just let it be, okay, Mom?"

"If you think so," she amended.

"Yes. I do." He exhaled slowly. Crisis averted, for now.

He got out of his SUV and knocked on Nicole's door. Her crazy was definitely rubbing off on him. Why else would he plant a kiss on her and then invite her to church yesterday? He should be trying to make her feel lonely, so she'd move back to Calgary and leave the way open for him to convince his parents to sell. Yet here he was, picking her up for church, hoping she'd like it. It made no sense. Even if he were to admit that he liked her, he should still want her to move to Calgary closer to where he lived.

He hadn't been able to forget that kiss from the night before, and when she opened the door, he had to fight the zing all over again. Wrapped in a black wool coat, with her dark hair framing her face and those beautiful eyes watching him expectantly, she couldn't be more adorable if she tried. A warm flush surged through him.

"Good morning." She smiled up at him, her cheeks pink.

"Good morning." He offered his arm for her to take.

"So where are we off to this morning?" She took his arm and allowed him to lead her to the SUV.

"Home Church, in Red Deer." He opened the back door for her.

"Oh. Is that one of those little church groups that meet in someone's house?"

"No." He chuckled, watching her slide into the back seat. "We're a little bigger than that. You'll see."

NICOLE STOOD between Garrett and Corrie as the last song ended. His strong baritone had been easy to listen to, and the pastor's message had been encouraging.

He hadn't been kidding about the size of the church. There were several hundred people in this service alone, and several services every Sunday, but everyone had been so warm and friendly. The whole experience had been wonderful. From the happy smiles of the folks directing traffic in the parking lot, to the cheerful people greeting newcomers and old friends with equal warmth in the lobby, the congregation had all lived up to their name and made this place feel like 'home'. She could easily see herself fitting into this church family.

They turned and collected their coats from the chair backs as the closing remarks were made.

"I'm going to sign up for The Christmas Experience," Corrie announced.

"What's that?" Nicole asked.

"That's a big Christmas party we host here for the community every year. We have sleigh rides, and quads pulling sleds for the kids to ride on. There's a skating rink, tobogganing, hot chocolate, carolers, a live Nativity, and of course a Christmas play and pictures with Santa. Last year I brought a couple of the goats for the kids to pet, but I think this year I'll just man one of the hot chocolate stations." Corrie shrugged into her coat. "Garrett. Do you want to volunteer this year? You're usually not home to help."

"I guess I could. My clinic in Calgary isn't expecting me back until January. What do they need?"

"Everything. There's always room to help. We also have the 'Christmas Is For Everyone' project you could assist with."

"Which is?" Garrett said.

"That provides Christmas for anyone who's having trouble financially. You can buy a gift for a child, buy a food hamper, or sponsor a whole family with gifts and food. If you don't have extra cash yourself, you can volunteer to do the shopping, or gift wrapping, or to deliver the hampers before Christmas. It's one of the ways we try to show God's love to our community."

"I'll meet you both at the front door when you're ready to leave," Corrie said as she bustled away.

Garrett turned to Nicole. "Want to help?"

"Yes. I'd love to." She grinned up at him.

"You're enthusiastic." Garrett returned her smile.

"Well, I usually go down to Arizona to spend Christmas with my snowbird parents. It's nice, but I'm just a guest there, so there's no place to fit in and help out. Since I'm home this year, this is a great opportunity to give back a little."

"I agree. Let's see what we can do." He took her hand and led her through the crowd to the volunteer table at the back of the sanctuary.

Nicole snuck a sideways glance at Garrett. He was so handsome in his black dress slacks and burgundy sweater. His hand felt strong and warm in hers, and the warmth spread through her, like a south wind, lifting her spirits and filling her with joy. This was going to be her best Christmas in years. She could feel it deep in her bones.

"Let's see. What should we do?" Garrett looked over the volunteer cards. "Why don't we sponsor a family? There's one here for a single dad with two little girls."

"I, uh. I'd love to, but I'm a little short of cash these days," Nicole said. *Understatement of the year.*

"Why don't I pay for it, and you can help me shop and do the wrapping. Mom says I wrap gifts really well, for a five-year-old."

Nicole burst out laughing. "Deal. Can we bring a couple of goats in for The Christmas Experience, too?"

"Really? You want to stand outside with some goats, in the freezing cold, for several hours, just so strangers can pet them?"

"Yes." She wrapped her arm around his, leaned in close, and looked up into his face, trying to make the biggest puppy-dog eyes she could. "Pleeese." She drew out the word and fluttered her lashes.

She could see Garrett's resolve melt away in the onslaught of her feminine power.

"Oh, all right." He cracked a lopsided smile. "You really know how to work those eyelashes don't you?"

"Maybe." She grinned up at him. "So, why are you usually not here for Christmas? Calgary isn't that far way."

"I usually volunteer with Doctors Without Borders for six weeks in November and December. We go and do free medical care in different places around the world. I had to come home early this year, because of Dad. I wasn't sure he was going to pull through, at first. I'm still not sure how much function he will be able to regain."

"I'm sorry about your dad. I hope he gets well again."

"Thank you. Me too."

"Now what?"

"Home, I guess."

Corrie had other plans.

CHAPTER TWELVE

*G*arrett stood outside his father's hospital room feeling like the biggest coward on the face of the planet. He was a doctor for heaven's sake. He'd spent many long days working within hospitals, checking up on his patients, doing rounds, and chatting with fellow staff. He'd always felt right at home. Now, here, his stomach clenched, and his palms were slick with sweat, just because it was his own father on the other side of the door.

Corrie had taken Nicole with her, off to the cafeteria to pick up some lunch, forcing Garrett to spend a few minutes alone with his father. They wouldn't be long. Time to man up.

He took a deep breath, straightened his spine, and stepped into the room.

"Hey, Dad. How are you doing?" The frail person lying on the bed was a far cry from the robust farmer his father used to be. Garrett's heart ached.

His father turned his head at Garrett's greeting. The smile

was lopsided, but it was there. Garrett let out the breath he had been holding without realizing it.

Abram Pine motioned with his one hand, so Garrett moved in closer, and took a seat in the chair beside the bed.

"I'm sorry it took me awhile to come back in." Garrett looked down at his hands, searching for words. "Honestly, I didn't know what to say." He looked up and met his father's gaze.

Abram nodded slightly, whether to agree, or to encourage him to say more, Garrett wasn't sure.

"I know your doctor. He's a good man, very smart and capable. I know you're in good hands. You don't need my medical care…So, I'm not sure you really need me here at all…" He trailed off.

Abram scowled, lopsided again, and shook his head as if to disagree. He tried to speak, but the words were garbled.

"I'm trying to help Mom out on the farm. I got her some hay, and I've been checking over some of the equipment. I'll arrange to have the machines serviced over the winter, so they'll be ready for planting season come spring."

Abram nodded. What Garrett saw broke his heart. Where was the big powerful man that had been his father? Replaced by this frail person, unable to speak or walk, half his body unresponsive.

At least it was the side with the missing hand that was affected. His left side, his only hand, still functioned normally. That was a blessing, of sorts.

Thinking of the missing hand, and the accident that had caused it, brought the usual rush of guilt and shame. If he hadn't been so selfish…If only he could rewind time, undo the mistakes that had led to that accident, be a better son.

He couldn't change the past. But he could certainly be a better son now. He could get his parents moved into someplace safer and make up for everything he'd done wrong. Life would be easier for them.

"I know I let you down before, Dad. I wasn't there when you needed me, but I'll do better now," Garrett continued.

Abram frowned and tried to speak, but it made no sense.

"Mom isn't agreeable yet, but I'll get through to her soon. I'll see you both set up somewhere really nice. You'll see."

"He'll see what?" Corrie asked, walking into the room.

"Nothing. We were just chatting," Garrett evaded. He stood up, relinquishing the chair for his mother to use.

Seeing Nicole peeking in from the hallway, Garrett motioned for her to come in.

"Dad, this is Nicole Mitro. She's renting the old house on the farm for now. Nicole, this is my father, Abram Pine."

"Hello." Nicole walked past Garrett and took Abram's good hand in her own. "It's so nice to meet you. You have such a lovely family. I'm enjoying getting to know them very much."

She bent down and whispered something that Garrett couldn't hear. He saw his father crack a crooked smile and wink at her in response. Now what was that about?

Nicole stood back up, blushing.

"I wish I'd brought my own car," Corrie said. "That way I could have stayed longer to visit. I don't want to hold you young people up though."

"Actually," Nicole offered, "Garrett and I could go shopping. We have some gifts to buy for the family we're sponsoring. We could call from the parking lot when we're ready to pick you up."

She looked at him. "Is that okay?"

"Yes. That's fine with me. Mom?"

"That would be perfect," Corrie replied. She reached over and took Abram's hand in her own. The love Garrett saw reflected between the two of them tightened his chest. Maybe one day, he could have that, too. A love so complete, that illness or infirmity couldn't diminish it. A love that only deepened with time. Maybe one day, after he'd fixed the mess he'd made.

He glanced over at Nicole and saw the look on her face as she watched the affection between his parents. She saw it, too. She hugged herself tightly, eyes glassy with unshed tears. She looked up at him, as if sensing his scrutiny. Their eyes met and held. Zing.

Maybe.

One day.

"This is perfect," Nicole cooed, holding up a pretty baby doll. "Let's get one for each of the girls and some of these cute little outfits, too."

"Maybe we should get one for you, too." Garrett ducked back, laughing, as Nicole took a playful swing at him. His hands were full of shopping bags from the other stores they'd visited.

"You just stop," she said with a laugh. "These are for the girls."

"Are you sure? You seem pretty enamored," he teased.

"That's enough out of you, mister." She picked out a few outfits for the dolls and dropped them in the cart which already held a couple of cute stuffed animals, some books and games.

"I'm glad you came with me," Garrett said. "I've never seen so many toys in one place. I'd have been lost without you."

"Surely you've bought toys for your nieces and nephews?" Nicole said.

"Don't have any. I'm the oldest. My younger brother, Dawson, isn't married, and my sister, Jess, is still in university. She'll be home for Christmas break soon."

"Will you all get together for Christmas?" Nicole asked. A big family Christmas sounded like fun, and something she'd never had.

"Yes. What about you, since you're not going to Arizona this year? Are your parents coming up for the holidays?"

"No. Sadly not. I'll be on my own, I guess." That was a dismal thought. Somehow, she'd overlooked that obvious reality in all the business of moving and getting her life sorted out. She'd been in such a panic to get out of the city, that all other considerations had fallen by the wayside. The idea of being alone for Christmas left a pall on her spirit.

"No brothers or sisters to get together with?"

"No. I'm an only child." Nicole tried to smile, but it felt stiff on her face. "I'll be fine. It's just a day."

"You could join us," Garrett offered, transferring all his bags to his left hand.

"That's very kind of you." She hesitated. "I'd hate to intrude."

"You wouldn't be intruding." He took her hand in his and lifted it to his lips, with the briefest of caresses, and said, "Come. I'd really like that."

Nicole felt heat wash through her. Could she do that? Be in a house with a couple of strangers without having a panic attack? The couple she'd had so far were just embarrassing. Yet, to be part of a family for Christmas was so tempting, to be with Garrett, irresistible. "I - I'll think about it."

"Would it help if I told you Mom's a great cook?" He grinned at her and gave her hand an encouraging squeeze. "Are we ready to pay for this and get out here?"

"Definitely."

Sitting in the SUV outside the hospital, Nicole couldn't stop thinking about Abram and Corrie. They seemed so devoted to each other, in spite of the stroke, and the obvious accident that had stolen Abram's right hand.

"What happened to your dad's hand?" she finally asked.

Beside her, Garrett stiffened visibly.

"I'm sorry. I shouldn't pry."

"No… Maybe it'd do me good to get it off my chest." Garrett sighed loudly and leaned back in the driver's seat, staring straight ahead out the window.

"Off *your* chest? Were you involved somehow?" Nicole asked, curiosity piqued.

"No. And yes. It happened because I wasn't involved, and I should have been."

"I don't understand," Nicole prodded.

Garrett looked away from her, out the side window. "Dad lost his hand in a farming accident. About ten years ago. And it's all my fault because I wasn't there when I should have been."

"What happened?" Nicole whispered.

"It was inevitable. I was always that kid with his nose in a book. Never much help with the farm chores. Always had something better to do. Dad was forever riding my butt about being more helpful, and I tried to weasel out of as much as I could.

"At harvest time, everyone is supposed to pitch in and help get things done, even kids. Twelve-year-olds know how to drive giant combines through a field of wheat or barley. As you get older, you can take on more responsibility. Sixteen-year-olds are driving the grain trucks back and forth to the silos.

"But the older I got, the more I despised farm work. It was knowledge that interested me, books and learning. I started college, then university. I was on my way to becoming a doctor. I didn't have time to help out, or at least that's the excuse I gave them.

"Mid-summer is when the hay needs to be cut, dried and baled. They called and asked me to come out to help. I could have, if I'd wanted to, but I didn't. I made up some excuse, an exam or something. I can't even remember what I said now, but I remember God told me to go help."

"God told you?" Nicole interrupted. That was a curious thing to say.

"Well, yeah. It was more of a feeling, you know? Like a push. I knew I should help, but I didn't want to, so I ignored it."

"Then later I got that call from Mom."

Garrett ran his hand through his hair and leaned his head back on the headrest again. Nicole could see the wet streaks on his cheeks as he stared up at the roof of the SUV. His voice cracked as he spoke.

"Dad got his hand caught in the baler. If he'd been a weaker man, it might have pulled him in completely. He could have died, right there, alone in the field, but he was able to wrench himself back, and it only tore his hand off."

Only tore his hand off. Nicole covered her mouth with her hand. How horrible. She could see it in her head. The blood, the calls for help, the agony. Poor Abram.

"If I had been there, he wouldn't have been hurt… It's all my fault."

"Garrett." Nicole's heart ached for him. "You couldn't have known that would happen."

"I should have."

"That's not fair to yourself," she said softly. Why had his father left the baler running while he worked on it? Even she knew that was risky.

Garrett suddenly cleared his throat, sat up straight and wiped his sleeve quickly across his face. She followed his line of sight out the window to see Corrie walking briskly towards them across the parking lot. She watched him hide his sorrow, and appear completely cheerful by the time his mother opened the SUV door to get in.

Nicole settled back in her seat for the drive home. She turned her head away to look out the window, watching the snow-covered fields slide by. Tears welled in her own eyes as she thought of the accident, of Abram having his hand ripped from his body. How terrifying that must have been. How guilty Garrett must feel if he blamed himself for it.

A tear eased down her cheek. It wasn't Garrett's fault. Accidents happen. There was no way he could have known.

However the blame fell, it didn't seem to have affected the love Corrie had for Abram, or the way he felt for her either. Their devotion to each other had been beautiful to see. Nicole swallowed a lump in her throat. Maybe, one day, she'd find love like that, too.

She glanced briefly at the man driving beside her. He was handsome, smart, and had very deep feelings kept tightly controlled. What would it be like if he let them loose? Let them loose for her?

Abram had seemed to approve when she'd told him what she thought of his son. Would the son approve, too? Time would tell. And in the meantime, she'd show Garrett that with her around, Corrie and Abram would have no trouble at home.

CHAPTER THIRTEEN

*N*icole poured a scoop of sweet feed into Mistletoe's feed pan and reached over the stall wall to scratch her back as she ate. The poor girl was definitely pregnant. You could see the little feet inside her belly push out here and there as she stood eating. With all the extra feed Nicole was giving her, the bony protrusions of her spine and hips were slowly padding over as she gained weight, but her belly was even larger than before.

Nicole smiled to herself, filled with happiness at the doe's improvement. She was so looking forward to the arrival of Missy's baby, too. Her first ever baby goat. The anticipation was palpable.

"Hello. I thought I saw you come in here," Garrett said, closing the barn door behind him and walking towards her.

"Hi, there," she answered. "I'm just checking on Missy. It's been two weeks. She should be okay to turn out with the other girls now, shouldn't she? She's been de-wormed and everything and isn't sick."

Garrett came to stand beside her and leaned over the box-stall wall to examine the goat. He smelled delicious as usual, his cologne overriding the background smells of hay and manure that pervaded the barn. Nicole inhaled deeply and felt a new warmth in spite of the deep chill in the barn.

"I don't think that would be a good idea," he said.

"Why? I just feel so bad for her. She's all alone in here, except for that lame cow across the aisle. But she has no goat friends."

The mentioned cow regarded them with large brown eyes, belched up a mouthful of cud, and began chewing thoughtfully. She mooed softly, her breath creating a plume of steam in the air.

"Not for long." Garrett chuckled.

"What do you mean? Is she?"

"Pretty soon. Look at that udder. She's all bagged up." Garrett pointed at the huge udder the doe had developed.

"What does that mean?"

"It means her milk has come in. It means she could give birth any time in the next week. How long has her bag been big like that?"

"I don't know," Nicole confessed. "I haven't really been paying attention to it. I didn't realize it was important." She bit her lip. Now what? She had no idea what to do. "What do I do? I've never helped a goat deliver before."

Garrett chuckled. "First, don't panic. The goat has the hard job, and they usually do fine all by themselves. You'll likely come in one day and find a couple of kids nestled in the straw beside her."

"A couple? You mean like twins? Oh, my goodness! How cute would that be?"

"Goats usually have twins. Sometimes only one, but I've heard of triplets and quads, too."

"Quads?" Her mouth dropped open.

"Hopefully not, or you'll be bottle feeding at least one of them. Missy probably won't have enough milk for four kids. Better hope for just one or two."

"What do I do? What do I need? I'm totally not prepared for this." Nicole began to pace, hands pressed to her cheeks. *What if Missy had trouble? What if the kids got stuck? What if there were too many?*

"Calm down. I'll drive you over to the farm store to get some emergency supplies. It will be fine. We'll just put some extra straw in her stall, just in case."

"Just in case what? You mean she could give birth now? Before we can get back?" Nicole's voice squeaked.

"Calm down," Garrett repeated, placing his hands on her shoulders and smiling down at her. "It will be fine. I promise." He gazed down at her, his deep blue eyes warm. The corners of his eyes crinkled in amusement.

"You think so?" Nicole wasn't sure. So many things could go wrong. Looking up at him, it was reassuring to know he was there to help. He wouldn't let her down. She smiled tentatively back.

"Man, you're cute when you're flustered," he murmured, and dropped a quick kiss on her forehead before releasing her abruptly and turning away. "Let's go grab the straw, then get your supplies."

Stunned, Nicole watched him stride to the back of the barn to grab a small square bale of straw. He kept doing that; sneak attack kisses, in and out so fast she was left slack-jawed, unable to respond properly before he was out of reach. She vowed she was going to have to do something about that, and very soon, too!

GARRETT HELD the door open for her as she carried in her bags of necessities. She had goat bottle nipples, long plastic gloves, iodine disinfectant, milk replacer and colostrum, and some emergency medications. She dumped the bag on her kitchen table, knocking a stack of mail all over the floor.

"Oops!"

"Never mind. I've got it." Garrett bent to gather up the scattered envelopes.

"Hey. What's this?" He held out a large post card.

"Nothing." Nicole snatched it out of his hand and shoved it in her back pocket where it began to burn a hole through her butt cheek.

"It looked like an invitation," Garrett pressed, arms crossed in front of him.

"It was… But I don't want to go." She *really* didn't want to go. In fact, the mere thought had her stomach twisting and giving her cramps. What if *they* were there? But that was ridiculous. Why would they be there? She probably *should* go. It was an honor. Her students would be disappointed if she didn't. She started pacing the floor. She should go. She should. She didn't want to. She'd been ignoring that invite for weeks. How'd Garrett manage to zero in on it?

She turned to find Garrett watching her intently. Her face heated and she cleared her throat. "It's nothing. Really."

"Right." He didn't sound convinced.

She nearly jumped out of her own skin when her phone rang and vibrated the table where she'd tossed it.

"Hello?" She answered automatically.

"HELLO." She pulled the phone away from her ear, cringing.

Speak of the Devil... It was Fred Allistar, Dean of Art at the college. Just the guy she'd been dodging. Nicole sighed. "Hello, Fred. How are you?"

"Fine. Fine. More importantly, how are *you,* Nicole?" Fred's voice boomed out of the phone. Fred's voice always boomed. She thought perhaps he was a little deaf and didn't realize it. She kept the phone away from her ear to protect her hearing a little. Out of the corner of her eye she saw Garrett smirk.

"I'm fine, Fred. Doing much better, thank you."

"Good. Good. So that means we'll be seeing you at the faculty Christmas party this Saturday then?"

Nicole's stomach dropped. "Um... I..." she glanced up at Garrett. He was studying his cuticles intently.

"I really don't think I can make it..."

"Nicole. You *have* to come. You're up for an award. Your students are planning to present it to you. You have to be there. They'll be so disappointed if you don't come," Fred cajoled.

"I don't know... Isn't it too late? I mean for the caterers. Didn't they need numbers last week?"

"Oh, don't you worry about that." Fred laughed so loudly

Nicole pulled the phone a little farther from her ear. "The students from Hospitality are doing the catering. They always make enough food to feed a Roman legion! There'll be plenty for you and your date."

"Date? I don't have a…"

Garrett took the phone right out of her hand. "Don't worry. We'll be there. See you then."

"Wonderful!" Fred boomed. "Fantastic! See you then." And he was gone.

Nicole gaped at Garrett.

"That guy is *loud*. Sorry, but I heard every word." Garrett held her phone out to her.

"What exactly do you think you're doing?" she demanded. Of all the nerve!

"Taking you to your party."

"And why would you presume to do that?" Nicole fumed.

"They obviously want you to be there. It sounds very important. And you just as obviously are terrified to go alone." Garrett sat with his back to the kitchen table looking unrepentant.

"How did you know that?" Was it written on her face?

"Well, first you were trying to hide the invitation, then you went white as a sheet when he started pushing."

Nicole stood glaring at him.

"Look. If you really don't want to go, don't. But it's Christmas. It's a party. You're up for an award. It'll be fun. You should go."

"I don't know…" It probably would be fun. She'd always had a good time before.

"Why not? What's got you spooked?" Garrett asked.

"Something happened," Nicole hedged, chewing her lip.

"At the college?" Garrett pressed.

"No... At home... but..."

"Want to talk about it?" Garrett asked.

"Maybe..." His face was calm, reassuring. Would he understand? Or not... "Maybe later."

"About that party, then. I bet your students miss you. I know I would." He winked at her.

She smiled, just a fraction, and rolled her eyes.

"So how about it? Will you do me the honor of allowing me to escort you to your party Saturday night?" He stood as he spoke, took her hand in his, and kissed its back while bowing a fraction.

Nicole couldn't help but laugh. "Well. When you put it that way... I'd be delighted."

CHAPTER FOURTEEN

*N*icole clutched onto Garrett's arm as they stepped into the college art gallery together. He smiled down at her and gave her hand on his arm an encouraging squeeze. She glanced up at him, so incredibly handsome in his tailored black suit, white shirt and Santa-red tie. It was quite the coincidence that his tie matched her evening gown perfectly. She held on a little tighter and looked around the room.

The gallery had been completely transformed for the Christmas party. Tables had been set up covered in red and gold tablecloths and adorned with poinsettias as centerpieces. Streamers and balloons hung from the ceiling, along with randomly positioned sprigs of mistletoe. A mix of traditional carols and modern holiday songs carried through the room without overpowering the conversations humming in the background.

The Hospitality students had outdone themselves. The buffet tables were piled with food and bowls of punch. The food smelled divine as it wafted across the room. Beside her, Garrett's stomach growled.

All the guests looked relaxed and happy, busily chatting away to friends and colleagues dressed in their Christmas finery. It looked so…normal. And yet…

Nicole pressed in closer to Garrett as she stared, wide-eyed, around the room. Irrational fear flooded her. Who was it? She knew it was someone aware of the schedule at the college. She searched the faces spread out before her. Who'd betrayed her? Attacked her in her own home? Were they here now? Her throat tightened and her pulse soared.

"I've changed my mind. I'm leaving." She dropped his arm, spun on her heel and hurried toward the door.

Garrett caught her in two strides. He took hold of her shoulder with one hand, slowing her forward movement.

"Nicole… Nic." His voice was calm, soothing, like balm on a raw wound. "It's safe. You're safe. It's okay."

She was shaking now, breathing in quick rapid gasps. The room seemed to darken, to close in around her. She gripped her purse, her fingers white with the strain. He eased her around to face him and softly pulled her closer, let her rest her forehead on his chest. She just stood there, quivering. He slowly ran his hands up and down her arms, whispering quiet words, drawing her back to reality.

Finally, she took a long, shaky breath, closed her eyes, and let the fear seep out of her, a bit at a time. When she had calmed, he placed his palm on the small of her back, and gently guided her back around towards the party.

"I'm right here. I won't leave you."

His hand was warm and reassuring on her back, but her

heart didn't slow. If anything, it sped up at the sensations his palm was causing; a warm curling deep inside her, racing tingles up and down her spine. He was right beside her, as promised, close enough to smell every delectable note of his cologne. She inhaled deeply, letting the warmth of his hand and the familiar scent steady her.

"It's going to be okay. I've got you," he said huskily.

And she believed him.

"Let's get you something to drink."

Unable to speak, she just offered a tremulous smile, and nodded. He guided her across the room to the cash bar that had been set up in the corner.

They ordered drinks and chose seats at a table with some of her favorite colleagues. Nicole draped her coat over the chair back to save her seat, then they began a slow circle of the room, greeting students and colleagues alike, sharing stories and laughter until the meal was ready to be served.

Nicole's level of panic eased off as the evening progressed. Of course, no one accosted her. It was a Christmas party, for heaven's sake. She felt foolish for getting herself so worked up earlier.

Garrett charmed everyone they met. They were enthralled by his stories from Mexico, and some of his escapades in Africa. Nicole noticed the admiring glances and a few openly jealous stares from her female colleagues. And why not? The man had beauty and brains. He was definitely the catch of the evening. Nicole kept a tight hold of his arm, drawing reassurance off the steady strength she found there.

Despite of the warm spirit of the evening, she couldn't quite shake the feeling she was being watched. Ridiculous of course. The room was full of people. It only stood to reason some of them would be looking her way. Still, when the music played the line, "He sees you when you're sleeping, he knows when you're awake…" It gave her the shivers.

That was kind of creepy, if you looked at it the wrong way. She hugged Garrett's arm just a little tighter. As long as he was there, it would all be okay.

GARRETT PUSHED BACK from the table and stretched his legs out in front of him. The food had been delicious and, just like Fred had promised, there was plenty to go around. Aside from Nicole's panic attack when they'd first arrived, everything had gone smoothly. Her friends had been happy to see her and had readily included Garrett in their conversations.

He glanced at the beautiful lady beside him, chatting animatedly to her friend. Nicole's glossy dark hair brushed across her bare shoulders, bouncing and swaying as she spoke. Her luscious red lips almost stopped his heart every time she smiled. Their color matched that of the strapless evening gown which clung to her slight curves, accentuating her petite frame.

The swash of bare skin across her shoulders begged him to touch it, caress its soft perfection, but he resisted. This was a first date after all, and she was in a pretty fragile state of mind. No need to push things. Besides, there was still the issue of selling the farm and convincing her to come back to her job here in Calgary. That shouldn't be too hard to do given how much fun she seemed to be having here tonight. Maybe they could be in Calgary, together.

When they were both back living in the city, well, who knows what might happen?

"Will you excuse me for a few minutes? I just have to run to the ladies' room. I'll be right back," Nicole said, standing up beside him.

A smile lit her face, and Garrett felt his heart catch a little in his chest. Lord, she was beautiful. "I'll be here." He was glad he'd made her come. He hadn't seen her smile this much since he'd met her. She just needed her confidence back, that was all.

NICOLE STROLLED PURPOSEFULLY through the crowded gallery, weaving between clusters of people, heading for the washrooms. Dinner had been fantastic, but nature called, and she needed to touch up her lipstick. She waved at a friend as she walked, then pulled to a sudden halt.

"Oh! I'm sorry. I almost walked right into you," Nicole apologized. The young man in the waiter's uniform had appeared out of nowhere right in front of her.

"I'm sorry about that, Ma'am. My fault. It's me. Tim Cardston. From your Art History class. Remember?" He shuffled his feet, while holding a half-empty tray of dirty glasses in front of him.

"I'm sorry, Tim. No. I have so many of you guys in that class I don't really remember individuals unless you've come to my office for help...*Did* you come to my office for help?"

Nicole racked her brain but didn't remember the kid at all. His voice was kind of familiar, but she couldn't pin it down. He was a nondescript kid, with lanky brown hair and bad skin. That could describe half the students in the college.

"No? That's okay. I was just wondering…Where'd you go? Your class has had a sub for weeks now." He transferred his tray to the other hand.

"Oh… That… It's, um. I just needed some personal time." She didn't want to explain it, especially to a student. A feeling of wrongness began creeping up her spine, but she pushed it away. She was just being silly again.

"Oh. Okay. When are you coming back?"

"I'm not sure, Tim. Why the interest?" *You're creeping me out, Tim. Why do you care so much?*

"We were just worried about you. We have a 'Get Well' card. I could bring it over to your house," he offered.

"Oh - That's so sweet of you…But you don't have to deliver it. I mean, if you have it here you could just give it to me." *What a jerk you are, Nicole, being all suspicious and he just wants to give you a card.*

"No. Sorry. It's not here. I left it at home. I was going to drop it by your old place, but the school admin said you'd moved."

"Yeah. I did. About three weeks ago."

"You sure I can't just drop it off for you? I don't mind," Tim pressed.

"No. It's too far for that. I'll pick it up next time I'm in town. Just leave it in my department mailbox. And thank you. That's very nice of you."

"I could mail it to you, if you give me your address."

Nicole hesitated. He sure was determined. Hopefully he put that much effort into his assignments. "I guess that would be okay. Send it to Nicole Mitro, RR2, Innisfail." She told him the postal code and noticed the pinch between his brows.

"Just a rural route number? You don't have a house address?" He seemed bothered by it.

"That's right. But don't worry. I'll get the card. All my mail arrives just fine. The landlady's son even delivers it to my door." *Like I'd give you my actual street address. The mailing one is good enough. You don't need to know where I actually live, buddy.*

"You see him much? The landlady's son? Is he there often?" Tim loosened the tie at his neck with one finger.

"Off and on. Why do you ask?" Nicole tamped down her impatience. She needed the restroom soon. Nature's call was becoming more demanding.

"No reason. Just hoping he's nice to you. That's all." Tim wiped his palm on his pants before shifting the tray to that hand and wiping the other palm on the other pant leg.

"He's very nice. He brought me here this evening. You don't have to worry about me. Now I have to get going, but it's been nice talking to you." Nicole smiled warmly.

She hurried off to the washroom, not waiting for Tim to try to say more. What a persistent kid. Nice enough on the surface, but still kind of creepy.

arrett reclined in his chair watching Nicole weave
her way through the crowd and out of sight. He
waited for a few minutes, then, feeling restless, rose
to his feet, stretched and began to stroll around the gallery,
looking at the art on display. Various paintings and drawings
hung on the walls, from simple line sketches to complex
multimedia works. Some pieces Garrett loved, others left him
scratching his head, wondering who on earth would ever want
to have something like that in their home. There were
sculptures, carvings, and ceramics positioned around the room
as well.

He was examining an interesting stone sculpture when one
of the waiters approached with a tray of desserts.

"Square?" The waiter held out his tray.

"Thank you." Garrett selected one that looked like a mix
of strawberry and cream.

"Enjoying the evening?" the waiter asked.

"Yes. The food was excellent. Thanks." He took a bite of his square.

"Oh, good. I'll let my classmates know the meal passed inspection."

"More than just a 'pass' I'd say. Probably worth an 'A'. Maybe 'A plus'."

"Thanks." The kid smiled but didn't seem as thrilled about the praise as Garrett would have expected. Kids these days. Who could understand them?

"I see you're here with Ms. Mitro," the waiter said.

"Yes. You know her?" Garrett asked.

"I'm in one of her classes. Um…do you know when Ms. Mitro is coming back? I'm…some of the students are anxious to see her again." He shifted his weight back and forth between his feet.

"I'm not sure. She hasn't said. Not before Christmas though." Garrett checked his watch. Where was she?

"Where's she gone to? We'd like to come by. Visit her. You know? We have a card." He licked his lips, still shuffling his feet.

"You'd better ask her yourself," Garrett answered.

"Right… I see you're checking out the art. Have you seen any of Ms. Mitro's work? She's really good."

"Some. Is there more here?"

"She has some pieces on display in the 'sale' gallery. I could show you," the waiter offered. "It's just in the next room."

"Lead on," Garrett said. Now this could be interesting. Her paintings at home had only been half finished when he'd seen them, but he'd liked them nonetheless. He was intrigued to see some of her finished work. He followed the young man out the door and down the hall into another large gallery.

"All the pieces in here are for sale. Some have been created by students and others by staff. I'll show you Ms. Mitro's. They're over here."

Garrett followed the young man around a corner to a wall where several paintings of various sizes were displayed. He smiled, warming to the works instantly. He could see her style all over them. They were all good, but there were two he loved. The first was a fall scene and depicted several deer grazing in a freshly cut field, with the early morning sun sparkling off frosted stubble. He loved the way she'd created the sun-glinting-off-ice effect. The scene gave him the feeling of serenity.

The second painting depicted mid-July in Alberta, showing a canola field in full bloom, a sea of bright yellow flowers glowing in the setting sun under a massive black thundercloud. The contrast of brooding, dark sky to vibrant, yellow ground was spectacular. How often had he driven past such a scene on the road, and wished his camera could capture the full magnitude of the view? There was a sense of beauty and foreboding in the calm before the storm unleashed its fury. His camera always failed, but here, Nicole had captured it perfectly.

He was awed. "These…These are amazing."

"Nice, huh? You could buy one. It would make a great Christmas gift."

"That it would." But which one? He loved them both. "Let's see. Is that the price?"

"Yes, Sir."

Pricey, but worth at least double that, maybe triple. The paintings were fantastic, and the fact that the artist was pretty fantastic didn't hurt either. "I'll take this one…and that one."

"Both?" The waiter sounded surprised. "Wow. Okay."

"Yes. Both," Garrett confirmed. "But I don't know how I'm going to get them home. I don't want Nicole to see what I've bought."

"No problem, Sir. For a little gas money, I can deliver them for you." His smile was broad, almost relieved.

"That's very helpful of you. So how does this work?"

The young man pulled a card out of a holder on the wall, one for each painting, and handed them to Garrett. "Just call the number here for the Art Department. Tell them you'd like to buy these two paintings. The painting ID numbers and names are on the cards. Then you can pay for them by credit card over the phone and tell them I will be picking them up for you."

"That sounds easy enough. Thanks for the offer."

"You're welcome, Sir…I just need the address now…"

"Right. Of course." Garrett found a stack of advertisement cards for the gallery and wrote down his parents' address and directions to the farm on the back of a card.

This was going to be great. He'd gift the field of deer to his parents for their living room. The glowing field of canola was all his, though. It would be the perfect bright spot of color in his own living room.

He turned to leave, then paused and swung back. "I almost forgot. Who do I tell them is picking up the paintings?"

"Tim. Tim Cardston."

"Great. Nice running into you, Tim."

"My pleasure, Sir."

NICOLE'S HEART raced and she struggled to control her breathing. Where was he? He'd said he'd be waiting. Sure, she had taken longer than she'd planned. But that Tim guy had delayed her on her way to the washroom, and another student had waylaid her coming out. By the time she got back, Garrett was no longer at their dining table.

She frantically scanned the room. Was that him? No. Too short. There? No. Too bald. He wouldn't leave without her. No, of course not. Would he? She clutched her purse so tight her fingernails were leaving dents in the leather. She needed him. He'd promised. That encounter with Tim earlier had left her unsettled. She needed his calming presence.

Finally. There, strolling through the crowd towards the dessert table, was Garrett. Nicole's breath escaped in a whoosh. She gulped a few deep breaths and let them out slowly. Garrett looked up, scanned the room, saw her, and smiled. Then he was walking her way, in a slow confident stride. Relief had her grinning like the Cheshire Cat.

"Hello, Gorgeous. What took you so long?" He planted a brief peck of a kiss on her cheek, then stood back, coffee in one hand, smiling down at her.

"I'm sorry. People kept stopping me to talk, then I couldn't find you," Nicole confessed. Gorgeous? Had he really just called her that? A warm glow spread through her, lifting the panic and pushing it away.

"Don't be sorry. When I got bored, I took a bit of a stroll to look at some of the art. I didn't worry you, did I?"

"No. Of course not," she lied. Not worried. Terrified more like. But she was better now. All it took was his presence to calm her racing heart and warm her soul. It was almost like she... *Whoa! Don't go there, girl. You haven't known him that long. Change the subject, quick.* "Do you like art?"

"Some of it. Some is just...bizarre."

Nicole laughed. "Well, I can't argue there. Art, like beauty, is in the eye of the beholder. What one person loves, someone else will hate. Did you find anything that you loved?" *There's that 'L' word again. Stop it, Nicole. Just* stop.

"One or two pieces caught my eye." He smiled like the cat who'd eaten the cream and took a sip from his cup.

Nicole was about to press him for details, when Fred Allistar's voice blared out over the PA system.

"HELLO! OH. Eh? This thing's LOUD isn't it?" Fred boomed into the microphone. "Someone turn down the volume. Heh, heh. That's better."

"Time for the awards!" he announced. "Everyone take your seats."

What followed was the routine, often dull, rounds of five-, ten-, fifteen-, and twenty-year service awards, a retirement announcement, a few lame jokes, with rare spots of true humor. Nicole feared Garrett was bored to tears, but every time she glanced his way he seemed to be listening with polite interest. Once he even caught her looking and winked. He must have been to his share of hospital Christmas functions over the years.

"And NOW," Fred boomed, "we come to the final award.

The 'Students' Choice' award for favorite professor... AND, the award goes to...NICOLE MITRO! Come on up here, Ms. Mitro."

Blushing furiously, Nicole stood and walked to the front amid cheers and applause. A few of her favorite students stood beside Fred, grinning away, holding a bouquet of flowers and a framed certificate. She accepted her flowers and shook hands with each of her students in turn. Back at their table she could see Garrett grinning broadly and clapping along with the rest. Pressed to say something by Fred, Nicole offered only a brief thank you to all her students before making her way back to her table.

Face flaming, Nicole took her seat. "That is so embarrassing. I hate being put in the spotlight. I must look like a tomato. My face feels ten shades of red."

"You look fantastic," Garrett replied, smiling warmly. "Besides, aren't you up in front of the class when you teach? I thought you'd be used to that."

"I'm only up front for Art History. The other classes are pretty much hands-on in smaller groups. I like those much better."

Things slowly wound down after that until Garrett said, "Time to go? We still have a ninety-minute drive to get home."

"Yes. I'm starting to fade."

There was still one thing on her agenda she hadn't mustered the courage to do yet, but her opportunity lay directly in their path ahead.

Garrett stood and held Nicole's coat for her to slip on, the same black wool felt she'd worn to church. It wasn't warm enough to spend long hours outside in January, but it was adequate for a short hike across the parking lot in December.

Nicole took Garrett's arm and allowed him to steer them through the thinning crowd towards the door. When they reached the doorway to the hall, she pulled them to a stop.

Garrett looked down at her. "Problem?"

"No. Not exactly a problem, or, at least I hope not." Nicole gazed up at him, not moving.

Garrett raised one eyebrow in enquiry.

Nicole smiled, feeling mischievous, and pointed up, over their heads, where a sprig of mistletoe had been hung. A slow sexy smile spread across Garrett's face when he caught her drift.

"I see," he said. "I hadn't noticed that little detail...You think we should do something about that?"

"Definitely," she replied huskily. And this time she'd make sure it wasn't a 'peck and run' kind of kiss.

Nicole tilted her head up as Garrett lowered his mouth to meet her lips. His kiss started soft, but quickly deepened, demanding more as she leaned in, matching his ardor with her own. Her fingers curled around the lapel of his wool overcoat as he placed his hands on her back, drawing her closer.

Nicole's heart soared as she took everything he offered. It was like she'd been starving but hadn't realized just how much until that moment. The smell of him, the taste of his lips, satisfied a longing she'd only now recognized. She had that exciting, terrifying rush one experiences when stepping onto a roller coaster.

Their lips parted, and she opened her eyes to see him staring at her, eyes a deeper blue than she'd ever seen, pupils dilated. The look he gave her sent her pulse racing. He started to lean back in, then...

"A-Hem! Excuse me. Coming through!" Fred announced at top volume as usual.

Nicole almost jumped back, feeling like an errant schoolgirl.

"You guys need a room? There's a group discount at the Holiday Inn tonight...In case you've been imbibing." Fred guffawed at his own innuendo and slapped Garrett on the back.

"That won't be necessary," Garrett answered stiffly.

Was his face red? It was hard to tell in the dim lighting. Nicole was sure hers was flaming. She took Garrett's arm, ducked her head, and let him escort her out to the car.

CHAPTER SIXTEEN

*N*icole sat snuggled in the passenger seat as Garrett drove them home. It had started to snow while the party was on and now, in the sub-zero temperature, tiny ice crystal snowflakes were blowing in the frigid wind. Curls of snow slithered and twisted like snakes across the pavement in front of them, until an oncoming car sent them airborne in a cloud of white powder.

Warm and snug inside, Nicole watched out the side window, seeing the Christmas lights strung across rooftops and along fence lines. The occasional person had gone all out, creating a Christmas wonderland with massive displays of lights and animated decorations for all to enjoy, but most kept it simple.

Despite the weather and road conditions, the SUV remained steady on the road, and Nicole relaxed, confident in Garrett's firm hand on the wheel. She must have dozed off, because the next thing she knew, they were pulling up in front of her house.

"Wake up, sleepyhead," Garrett teased gently.

Nicole sat up straighter, blinking like an owl, as she got her bearings. Garrett exited his side, and came around to open her door, and help her out of the car. Icy wind whipped her hair into her face, so she grabbed Garrett's arm, and let him walk her to the door.

"Thank you for a wonderful evening. I'm so glad I let you talk me into it. I'd never have gone on my own."

"The pleasure was all mine. I wouldn't have missed it." Garrett opened the door for her, and waited, holding it open.

"I'd invite you in, but…"

"It's late. And you're half asleep. And you have farm chores in the morning." Garrett shrugged. "But we're still on for Sunday, right?"

"Sunday?" Nicole was so tired, she felt like her brain was asleep already.

"The Christmas Experience. Remember? The big Christmas event at Home Church? You wanted to take a couple of the goats for the children to pet."

"Oh, right. Is that this Sunday already? I'm completely losing track of time. That means Christmas is just over a week away. Yes. Of course, I want to do that."

"All right, then. I'll pick you up about eight thirty so we can get there and set up in time. Sound good?" Garrett asked.

"Yes. I'll be ready."

"Good." He smiled lazily. "And when it's all finished, how about I take you out for dinner, just the two of us?"

"That - that sounds perfect."

"Then it's a date." Garrett leaned in, touched her chin and tilted her face up towards his, then kissed her, slow and sure, drawing it out, and curling her toes. "Good night," he whispered, and turned away, back to his idling car.

GARRETT SAT ALONE at the kitchen table, coffee in hand. The rich dark brew was slowly bringing him back to life. He took a sip and let the warmth snake down his throat. He contemplated making toast, then rejected the idea, preferring to sit, staring out the window. The sun was brilliant this morning, glittering off the snow, causing it to sparkle like a white blanket of rhinestones, creating a false expectation of warmth where there was none.

Garrett watched Nicole cross the yard doing her farm chores. Bundled in her warm parka, wearing her new insulated farm boots, with her knitted wool hat pulled low over her ears, she still looked cold. She carried two large pails from the house towards the chicken coop, likely topping up the water in the heated water bowls.

She was diligent, he'd give her that, insisting on doing the chores alone since it was technically part of her rent. He'd already watched her bring hay from the barn out to the goats, dragging it on a big orange calf sled. She'd fed Norbert first, walking through his pen as if he didn't outweigh her and couldn't break her knees if he chose to, and then she'd fed the girls, penned across the lane on the other side of her house. The girls had a heated automatic waterer, but Norbert would need his heated water bucket topped up by handheld buckets, when she'd finished with the chickens.

Nicole didn't complain about the work at all, the way

Garrett had as a teenager. She actually seemed to enjoy herself, stopping to scratch Norbert's head and talk to the chickens. She spent a long time in the barn, dealing with Missy, he assumed, and came out smiling.

Garrett scowled to himself. He'd been sure the novelty of farm life would have worn off by now, but she was proving him wrong, again. He recalled her stubborn, pig-headed refusal to ask for help moving all those bales of hay. She seemed determined to stay. Still… she'd seemed to have fun with her old colleagues last night. She couldn't hide out here on the farm forever. She'd need to go back to work eventually, and it was too far of a commute from here.

Thoughts of the previous evening banished the frown from his face. He'd told himself he was just trying to get her back to work, and over whatever it was that had spooked her but if he was being honest, he'd really wanted to see her all fancied up and having a good time. He hadn't been disappointed.

That red gown had fit like a glove, accentuating her tiny frame and showing off her sweet curves. His temperature rose just thinking about her, and the way her eyes sparkled when she laughed. Her wide generous smile, luscious in red lipstick, haunted his memory. He'd hardly slept all night, thinking of her, and the taste of her lips on his.

He stood up, restless and agitated. She seemed to be always on his mind, consuming his thoughts, an itch he couldn't scratch, a longing he hadn't yet acknowledged. He crossed the kitchen to pour another cup of coffee, then returned to the window to stand there and watch. Dark strands of hair blew across her face. She paused to brush them aside, tucking them under her hat, before disappearing into the barn again.

'I'll Be Home For Christmas' played softly on the radio. Garrett's throat tightened. He was at his mother's home, but didn't feel *at* home. Nicole, living in the little house he'd grown up in, seemed more at home than he did. His current home was a stark, cold apartment in the city, a place to sleep, but even that didn't feel like home.

He watched Nicole emerge from the barn and head home. *She* felt like home. Christmas would be over soon, and he'd be back in Calgary, in a bare apartment, far from his parents, brother, and Nicole. Surprisingly it was that last part that bothered him the most. Nicole. Not seeing her daily.

What was happening to him? He'd always been so independent, a loner. Now he couldn't bear the thought of returning to Calgary without her. But knowing her, and her kind compassionate heart, she'd not abandon his parents when they needed help with the chores.

Speaking of which, he watched as his mother's SUV turned into the lane and made its way up to the house to park beside his brother's pick-up truck. Knowing Garrett would be out late the night before, Corrie had asked his brother, Dawson, to drive her to the hospital earlier that morning. Their father was coming home today. Garrett wasn't sure that was a good thing, but Corrie wanted him home for Christmas.

Dawson parked, and came around to the passenger side of the SUV while Corrie emerged from the back seat. Dawson opened the door, and leaned inside to half lift Abram from the seat and help him to stand. Garrett's heart dropped, watching the slow shuffle as his father, leaning heavily on Dawson, followed closely by Corrie, made his way towards the house. Garrett opened the door for them as they approached.

"Hey, G-man. Coming through!" Dawson said.

Dawson, three years younger, an inch taller, and a bit broader across the shoulders, had been cheeky and disrespectful since they'd been teens, even to the point of never using Garrett's real name, preferring to call him G-man, or worse, Super-G. Garrett really hated that one. It usually got used when Dawson was mad at him for some imagined slight. Garrett bit his tongue, wanting to avoid a fight.

They'd been best friends when they were kids, always together. Dawson had followed him around like a puppy. They'd played in the barn, gone frogging in the creek, swimming in the dug-out, and both had played hockey, although Dawson had been in a younger division than Garrett. But then, somewhere in high school, Garrett had started hitting the books in his bid to leave farming behind, and Dawson had become argumentative and distant. The hazel eyes that had looked at him with admiration now held scorn. The stupid nickname was born. Garrett missed the little brother he used to have but didn't want to hang out with the smart mouth Dawson had become.

Garrett stepped back, making room for them to come inside. Dawson, holding firmly to their father's belt with one hand, walked Abram into the kitchen. Garrett pulled out a chair and held it firmly for Abram to sit in.

"How're you doing, Dad?" Garrett asked.

Abram gave him a 'thumbs-up' and, with a crooked smile, slurred, "Doin'…good."

"I have his cane here," Corrie said. "They wanted him to

use a walker, but it was just too awkward to use with only one hand." She propped it against the table beside him.

"B-be... fine," Abram managed to say.

Watching his dad, Garrett couldn't help but worry. How would they manage? At least their new home had the master bedroom and bath on the main floor, down the hall from the kitchen and living room. As a guest, Garrett was sleeping in an upstairs room, as would his sister, Jess, when she got home in a few days for Christmas break.

"Would you like some coffee, Dad?" Garrett asked.

At Abram's nod, Garrett walked towards the coffee pot. Dawson leaned up against the counter, arms crossed, long legs stretched out and butt resting on the counter edge, blocking access to the coffee.

Garrett paused, Dawson stared him down but didn't move. Garrett waited, but finally had to say, "Excuse me," before Dawson slowly moved out of his way. It was a constant battle of wills for reasons Garrett didn't understand.

Garrett poured a cup for his dad and carried it back to the table. Abram took the cup with his good hand and took a sip. A tiny bit of coffee trickled out of the right corner of his mouth. Corrie quickly dabbed the moisture away with a napkin.

Garrett turned away, unable to watch his father's infirmity.

"The occupational therapist suggested using a straw to drink with for a while. I'll get one. I'm sure I have some stuffed in a drawer somewhere." Corrie started rummaging through her kitchen drawers.

Heartbroken, Garrett stared out the window. If only his parents weren't so set on staying on the farm. They could have a good life in Calgary, near him. It was killing him to see his dad so frail. He couldn't just stand back and do nothing. Maybe if they understood how much they could get for the farm, and the nice places available in Calgary, they might see how good it could be for everyone. Then Nicole would be free to move back to her old job without feeling like she'd let them down, too.

That was it. He'd get a realtor over, get an estimate done. Then he'd have some real numbers to work with and they could have a serious conversation about this place. In fact, he'd go upstairs immediately and call around to set something up for this week.

Besides, no one would miss him. With Dawson present, all three members of his family had dropped into farmer-mode and were busy talking cows, calving and the price of canola. They wouldn't even know he was gone.

CHAPTER SEVENTEEN

*N*icole felt a rush of excitement as she and Garrett pulled into the overflow parking at the church Sunday morning. Today was 'The Christmas Experience'. They had awoken early to load two of their sweetest goats into a small stock trailer. Of course, Missy was the best of all, but she had to be left at home due to her advanced pregnancy, and the fact that they had no idea when she might go into labor. Xena and Beatrice had been chosen to go instead.

Nicole stepped from the truck, bundled in her warmest parka, hat and mitts. The new boots had proven invaluable at home, keeping her toes toasty warm through all her farm chores. Hopefully, they'd hold up for five hours of Christmas festivities in a northern prairie December.

Across the way a pair of draft horses were being hitched to a sleigh. Someone had created an ice rink for the kids to skate on, and someone else was setting up inner tubes to be dragged behind a quad. Christmas music played across the grounds from speakers on the church, and campfires had been lit around the grounds so people could warm up.

"This looks like it's going to be so much fun," Nicole said, grinning. The sun sparkled off the snow creating a glittering diamond effect.

"It usually is," Garrett replied. "Let's go get some hot chocolate now, before it gets busy."

"What about the goats?"

"They'll be fine in the trailer until we get back. Once the first performance of the play is over, we'll come out and lead them around for people to pet," Garrett said.

"Sounds like a plan."

Nicole followed Garrett to a hot chocolate station, then into the church building. Inside, Santa was setting up with several elf helpers for pictures, and around the corner on a carefully placed tarp, a live Nativity scene had been created complete with a real pony, a couple of sheep, and a living Mary, Joseph and baby. She and Garrett found seats, laughed through the play, and when it was over, made their way back outside to the trailer.

"You lead Beatrice," Nicole said, handing over the lead to the white goat. "I'll take Xena. Here's a baggie of treats to put in your pocket, so there's something for people to feed them."

"Good thinking. Ready?" Garrett asked.

"Let's do this." Nicole grinned at him. This was going to be her best Christmas ever. She could feel it.

Nicole never had so much fun. The children loved petting the goats, touching their horns, and especially having goats lick grain off their palms. The smiles and giggles were contagious. Even the parents and other adults enjoyed petting the goats. As for Xena and Beatrice, they licked their lips and wagged their tails with every treat they got.

"Look at her eyes!" A little girl squealed in delight. "They're so weird."

"But she has such a cute face," said another.

"She's so wooly!" remarked a small boy. There were hugs and goat kisses all around.

By three o'clock things were winding down, booths were closing and the hot dog Nicole had eaten earlier had worn off. Her tummy growled in complaint.

"I don't know about you," Garrett said, "but I'm starved. Time to call it quits. What do you think?"

"Agreed. I'm hungry, too. And my feet are killing me."

"Not frostbite again?" Garrett sounded worried.

"No. Just sore from walking around for hours," Nicole replied with a grimace. "Do we drive the girls home, then come back to eat?"

"No. I brought some hay, and a bucket. You load them up, and I'll get them some water. They'll be happy to eat in the trailer while we have dinner."

Not long after, Garrett found a side street to park on since the truck and trailer were too big to park in the lot. They chose a little Mexican restaurant in town, and spent a comfortable two hours enjoying their meal, talking and laughing.

The sun had already set by the time they emerged from the restaurant, leaving the sky in frigid blackness, dotted with tiny stars. Garrett had started the truck remotely from inside five minutes earlier, so Nicole was able to climb up into a warm cab in spite of the outside temperature. She buckled up and snuggled back into her seat as Garrett came around to the driver's side.

"There's no room to turn around here, so I'll just drive through this neighborhood to loop around back to the highway. It'll give us a chance to see some Christmas lights, too," Garrett said, buckling up his own seat belt.

Nicole just smiled agreement, feeling happy and content. It had been a wonderful day, her and Garrett together, helping contribute joy to The Christmas Experience. It felt great to give to others and make Christmas a happy time for everyone.

She couldn't believe how comfortable she felt with Garrett, especially knowing him such a short time. She thought she'd never be able to trust anyone when she'd first moved, but he'd won her over with his caring nature and quiet strength. It was obvious he loved his parents, and he must see by now that everything on the farm was running smoothly. She was there to help out, and there was no need for anyone to move. Hopefully he'd come out often to see them once he was back to work in January. Who knew where things might lead?

The truck turned a corner, and, in addition to the glow of Christmas lights, a more alarming red and blue glow throbbed up the lane. Nicole gasped as the memory hit her. She tensed, trying to control the surge of fear that assaulted her.

"What's wrong?" Garrett asked, a frown creasing his brow. "You've gone stiff as a board."

From the corner of her eye, Nicole saw him glance up the road to the approaching corner with the pulsing blue and red light, and then back at her. He turned the corner, and there they were, three cop cars, lights twirling on their roofs, two on the street and one in the driveway of a home, people in the yard, door open, movement inside.

Nicole clamped her eyes shut. "Just keep driving," she whimpered. "Please."

"Nicole? What's going on in your head? It's just a couple of cop cars. Nicole? Nic?"

"Just get us out of here. I can't breathe. Please." She infused her voice with the urgency ripping through her.

"Okay. We'll be gone in a second," Garrett reassured her.

The truck moved on, the glowing lights faded behind her closed lids. Nicole tried to slow her breathing, while cracking her eyes open to confirm they had left the area. They seemed to be on their way, but as the truck was passing a small city park, Garrett slowed and pulled over to the curb.

"Why are we stopping?" Anxiety thrust through her. "We have to get home. It's not safe here!"

"It's perfectly safe," Garrett said, his voice slow and calm. "See? There's no one even here. It's dark and freezing cold outside. There is no one out here but us."

"B-but those people might be heading this way," Nicole's voice rose in panic.

"What people? Nic? What people are heading this way?"

"I don't know!" She wailed, her voice louder, shriller. "Whoever broke into that house back there."

"What makes you think someone broke in? There's a dozen reasons police might have been called there."

She stared at him as if he were nuts. "Because… because…" She shrugged, hugging herself tightly, and looked away. She couldn't explain. She just knew, deep in her soul. She knew. Her body felt so tense, she thought she'd snap, like an overwound guitar string. She could feel herself shaking. That same feeling, taking over.

"Nic?" Garrett's voice penetrated the fog of panic surrounding her.

"Is that what happened to you? Nic?"

She couldn't speak. She just nodded, hugging herself even tighter.

"Tell me about it," Garrett pressed, his voice soft and compelling.

Nicole shook her head silently. A single tear coursed down her cheek and dropped off onto her jacket sleeve. She wiped it off with irritation.

"Nic? This will never leave you if you keep it trapped inside. You need to let it out. Let it go."

She looked at him then, seeing the earnest care on his face. Her vision blurred, and her throat tightened. She felt another tear trickle down her face.

"Do you like feeling this way?" he asked.

She shook her head. That was a stupid question. Of course not. But what choice did she have?

"Then you need to let it out," he insisted. "Tell me what happened. I know it helped when I told you about my father's accident."

He had trusted her with that, hadn't he? She hadn't blamed him for it. Maybe he wouldn't think her too stupid if she told him her story. "If you start driving, I'll tell you. Just get me out of here first."

Garrett stared her down a moment, then turned the engine over, and pulled away from the curb, heading towards the on-ramp, and the highway home.

Once they had merged onto the highway, Nicole began to speak, softly at first, but gaining strength as she went.

"I came home after work one day in early November. I wasn't feeling well, so I came home early when I was supposed to stay late for a fundraiser meeting."

Nicole allowed her mind to drift back, remembering.

NICOLE TRUDGED across the yard to the ground floor entrance of her basement suite in Calgary. Head pounding, she paused to cough deeply into her elbow before fumbling to get her key into the lock. Stupid cold. So much for the planning meeting at the college tonight. She ached all over. No meeting for her. Just a warm blanket on the couch, a cup of tea, and Netflix.

Shivering, Nicole coughed again before pushing open her door. She shuffled into her one-bedroom suite, dumping her art bag in the hallway by the door before kicking off her boots and struggling out of her winter coat. She was chilled to the bone, even now that she was inside, but maybe that was just the November wind. She'd have to crank the heat up, although she could already hear the furnace blasting hot air.

She tucked a strand of long dark hair behind her ear and was about to grab her bag when a low feline growl pierced through the fog of her misery. Norman, her landlord's cat, crouched by the door to the stairs, glaring up the stairwell.

"What are you doing down here, Norm?" she asked. She could have sworn she'd closed the door after feeding him that morning. She was cat sitting for a couple of weeks while her landlords were on vacation.

She heard a thump upstairs, and low voices. That was odd. She thought they weren't due home for a couple of days yet.

Nicole pushed the door open farther before calling out, "Hello? Mr. Fellows? I wasn't expecting you home yet. Is everything okay?"

Her query was met with silence.

"Mr. Fellows?" Nicole dragged herself up the stairs and poked her head above the railing.

Two male figures in black balaclavas stared back at her.

"You said she wouldn't be home!" one accused the other.

"She's not supposed to be!"

Nicole stared wide-eyed, her frantic heart hammering in her chest. It seemed to take forever for her brain to scream 'RUN'.

She did.

"Get her!"

She scrambled back down the stairs, taking them two at a time, with someone right on her heels. She hit the bottom of the stairs, swung through the door, and tried to slam it behind her. She was too slow. The door slammed back into her chest, sending her flying backwards across the hall into the bookcase. She hit the floor hard, then rough hands grabbed her arms. Still on her back, she kicked out wildly, catching the guy on the shins.

He cursed and made another grab at her. She kicked at him again, catching her foot on something around his neck, breaking it. She flailed wildly.

"Stop! Let's just get out of here. You said no one would get hurt," the other man said.

"She's seen us!"

"She hasn't seen anything important."

Nicole remembered her voice.

"HELP! RAPE! FIRE! HELP!" she screamed everything she could think of.

"SHUT UP!"

Her cheek exploded as he struck her. She cowered back, covering her face with both hands.

"Let's go. Let's go," she heard one say. And then there was silence.

Nicole lay curled in a ball on the floor, arms flung around her head, shaking violently. Waiting. Listening.

There was only the ticking of a clock on the mantle.

Norman crept over and lay down beside her, his soft purr vibrating his chest. She reached out, pulled him close, and buried her face in his fur.

A cold wind blew in the open door.

CHAPTER EIGHTEEN

*G*arrett realized his hands were starting to cramp from gripping the steering wheel so tightly. He was furious. Beyond furious. To break into her home? Then hit her? Her! A tiny little woman like his Nicole. If he could get his hands around that guy's neck…

"The worst part is," Nicole continued, "that it's all my own fault." Her mouth drooped with that admission.

"What are you talking about? No way getting robbed and then assaulted is your fault. No way."

"But I was stupid. Even the cops thought so," Nicole said forlornly.

"A cop called you stupid?" Now he was really getting mad.

"Well, he didn't actually use the word, but I could see it in his face later that night when they were collecting evidence."

Nicole continued her story.

CONSTABLE SMITH STROLLED OVER and handed her a baggie of ice and a cup of tea that he'd made for her in her kitchen. He sat down in a chair opposite the couch where she huddled, wrapped in a blanket. The paramedics had already been, and gone, declaring her bruised but not in need of a trip to the hospital. She held the ice to her cheek but left the cup on the coffee table. Her hands were still shaking too much to sip tea without spilling it.

"So, you're sure you don't know who did this?" he said again.

"I'm sure," Nicole repeated. How many times had they gone over this?

"But one of them definitely knew you, or at least your routine," he pressed. "Where were you supposed to be tonight?"

"I was supposed to be at a meeting for the college art department tonight, but I wasn't feeling well, so I bailed out and came home early. They must have thought I'd be there." Anxiety clenched her stomach. Who could it have been?

"I found something," a different officer said, holding out a tarnished gold chain in his gloved hand. "By the bookshelf."

"It's not mine," Nicole asserted. "It must belong to the one who hit me. My foot snagged in something as I was kicking at him. Maybe that's it."

Constable Smith examined the chain in the other officer's hand. "Cheap junk. Why bother wearing this?" He shrugged and said, "Just bag it for evidence."

"Has anything been taken from your place?" Smith continued.

"I don't think so…But I really haven't looked. I didn't

notice anything out of place when I came home, except that the door to upstairs was open and Mr. Fellows' cat was down here," Nicole added.

"Looks like they came in through the back sliding glass door. It's still open," the second officer commented from the kitchen.

"That door hasn't been latching properly for a while now. I've been complaining about it for months. Mr. Fellows keeps promising to fix it but..." Nicole trailed off.

"You've been complaining? To whom?" Smith asked, scowling down at his notepad.

"To everyone," Nicole admitted sheepishly. "I might have posted it."

"On social media?" Smith's eyebrows shot into his hairline. "Did you post that your landlord was going to be away, too?"

Nicole felt her face flush. From the look on Smith's face, she felt no need to further admit her foolishness. What an idiot she was.

"So that widens our suspect pool to...just about everyone." Smith scowled at his notes. "You were targeted. You shouldn't stay here alone tonight. Do you have somewhere else to go?"

"I... I'll call a friend for tonight."

Nicole scanned the room, saw the cracked door to the upstairs, her art bag shoved into the corner, the scattered knickknacks from the bookshelf where they lay smashed on the floor. She shuddered involuntarily. How could she stay here? How could she ever feel safe here again? And someone who knew her was responsible? Someone *she knew?*

How could she look at any of her colleagues? Who was the culprit? One of her co-workers at the college? A student? One of her *friends*? Those had been men's voices, to be sure, but who was to say that their information hadn't come from a girlfriend? Nausea curdled her stomach. She had to get away from here. She had to.

"AND THAT'S when I decided I had to move. Not just out of that basement suite, but right out of Calgary. Crime is getting worse and worse. There have been attacks on campus. It just isn't safe anymore," Nicole concluded.

"So you posted about the faulty lock on the door, and about your landlord being away?" Garrett probed.

"Yes. I'm such a moron."

"Probably not the smartest thing to do," he agreed. "But a lot of people do that all the time, so it's not like you're the only one." He realized she probably felt little consolation from that, but couldn't tell by her expression, since she kept her face turned out the window.

"Who knew about the department meeting that night?" he asked.

"I don't know. But I didn't post about that. It didn't seem that important," she said in a subdued voice.

"So it had to be someone associated with the college, likely someone in the art department," he concluded, glancing at Nicole while he drove. Those rats! If he ever got his hands on them…

Nicole nodded, misery etched into her face. "That's why I

was afraid to go to the Christmas party. I used to think they were my friends, but someone…someone set me up."

Garrett thought for a moment. "Look. Based on what you've said, that someone thought you wouldn't be home. It seems to me that they weren't planning to hurt you. If anything, they were trying to avoid you. They weren't even trying to steal from you. They were targeting your landlord upstairs."

Nicole remained silent for a minute, then admitted, "I guess you're right about that… Still. It was terrifying."

"I'm sure it was." Garrett reached across the truck and took her hand in his. It felt like ice. "But it's over now. You were strong. You survived."

"I suppose. I don't feel very strong. I just wish I knew who did it. Every person I see, I wonder, 'was it you'?" Nicole sighed, and squeezed his hand. "Thanks for not calling me a dummy."

Garrett squeezed her hand back before releasing it to turn into their driveway.

"Now you understand why I'm not working," Nicole continued. "I couldn't bear the thought of going to work, searching every face, wondering who it was that had assaulted me. I had a lot of unused sick leave accumulated, so I decided to use it and call it stress leave. I needed a break and some time to think about what to do.

"And you also know why I moved way out here. I didn't feel safe in my old place after the break-in. I couldn't sleep. I stayed in my parents' place for a month while I looked for a place of my own. They were already down in Arizona for the winter, so they didn't mind. It still felt scary there, all by myself, so when I saw your mother's ad for the little farmhouse, I jumped on it.

"I finally feel safe here. I never want to leave. You can understand that, can't you?" She turned her piercing gray eyes on him, and his heart constricted.

Guilt sucker punched him in the gut. He should tell her about the realtor. He should remind her that he wanted his parents to move to Calgary where he'd be able to look after them better. This was his chance to make up for his failure years ago. He needed to make things right.

But… that would upset Nicole. After all she'd revealed, he understood why…

He looked at her expectant face, waiting for reassurance from him. Even with her make-up smudged from crying, she was exquisite. The face of an angel with the heart of a lamb, soft and innocent and pure. With a tightening of his throat, he realized he didn't want to hurt her either. He couldn't bear the thought. Because…because… He was falling in love with her. The reality stunned him.

It was true. How could he not have seen it sooner? He loved her! His mind raced.

He needed time to think, to figure things out, to come up with a solution. So, yes, he needed to talk with her, but not tonight. She was exhausted, both physically and emotionally. Now was not the time to broach this subject. There'd be plenty of time to talk things over and come up with solutions after Christmas. This could wait. He had time.

"I understand completely," he assured her.

A smile bloomed on her face, piercing him to his soul.

"I knew you'd understand," she whispered, and leaned in, offering him her kiss.

He met her lips with his, cupping her head with his hand, drawing her closer. Her mouth was sweet on his, a wicked temptation. He submerged himself, opened his heart, allowed himself to feel, to drown in her kiss, and the feelings surging through him. Sinking in, lost in her presence, with total surrender, he let himself love her.

He couldn't think, couldn't plan. He just pulled her closer, crushed her mouth with his, and let the feeling surge. He came up for air, saw the look in her eyes from the porch light glow, and knew.

"Nicole," he breathed her name like a prayer. *I love you.* He wanted to say it so bad. He almost choked, holding it back. He needed to work things out first, so he bit his tongue.

She gazed up at him with pure joy on her face. He could almost convince himself she felt the same way. Maybe she did. He pulled her back in close, the hand brake between them only a minor irritation as he kissed her thoroughly until she was as breathless and surrendered as he.

With a massive effort of will, he finally pulled back. Her cheeks were flushed, and her pupils dilated. Her lips parted, soft and moist, and slowly curled into a satisfied smile. He almost pulled her back in for more, but duty and honesty compelled him to set things straight before going too far.

"It's going to all work out," he murmured huskily. "I promise."

She cupped his cheek with her palm. "I think it just might."

"It's been an eventful day. Why don't I unload the goats,

and you get some sleep? Morning chores are all on you, okay?"

She nodded, with a satisfied little smile on her face, and slipped out of the car. She turned at her door, and waved good night before slipping inside and turning off the porch light.

It would work out. He'd make sure of it, because he finally understood the stakes. He'd call that realtor and postpone the estimate inspection first thing in the morning. He needed more time to figure things out, but there was one thing for sure. He loved that girl, and needed to keep her in his life.

CHAPTER NINETEEN

*N*icole floated through her chores the next morning joyously humming a carol. With only three days until Christmas Eve, and the sun sparkling off the snow in the piercing cold, she couldn't have been happier. The glow from last night had yet to wear off. He had been so passionate, yet so tender. Could it mean he had feelings for her? The same feelings coursing through her right now? Was it possible that he loved her? She felt like she was walking on air.

She'd told him everything, had come clean about her fears and foolishness, and he'd not thought her stupid at all. He'd been calm and strong and supportive. Best of all, he said he understood why she had to stay here. If he understood he'd never ask her to move now. Right? She was over the moon with happiness!

Nicole crossed the yard from the barn carrying a load of hay. She let herself into Norbert's pen, and carried the hay over to his feed rack while he sauntered along beside her. She and Norby had an understanding. As long as she didn't try to push him around, he didn't try to snag her leg with his horns. It was a respectful relationship, at least for now. Come fall, when the ladies came into heat, he would be too dangerous to mess around with. She'd have to talk with Corrie about moving his feeder close to the fence so she could fill it up from the outside before the fall rut started.

She gave him a little scratch under his chin then left his pen, locking the gate securely behind her. She never touched his forehead, since he might take that as a challenge. One tried to avoid challenging an animal far bigger and stronger than oneself, if at all possible. At least, smart people did. She'd already recovered from several bruises on her thigh where Norbert had suddenly swung his head towards her, digging one of his horns into her leg and dragging it across her flesh.

Nicole crossed back to the barn and slipped inside to its comparative warmth. As the door closed, and her eyes adjusted to the inner gloom, Missy bleated softly from her box-stall. Across the aisle the lame cow mooed her welcome amid a plume of steam.

Nicole grabbed some hay for Missy and filled her hay rack. Missy reached her head up over the half door for a scratch under her chin and along her neck. Poor girl looked wide as a cow, but still showed no sign of going into labor. It was so frustrating, not knowing exactly when she had been bred. It was impossible to know when she was due to give birth, so Nicole could only watch and wait and hope everything went well.

Nicole leaned against the stall door, watching Missy eat, and humming softly to herself. She couldn't get last night's kiss out of her mind. It had tingled her spine and curled her toes, that was for sure. And the look on his face afterwards? Wow! Just thinking about it, about him, sent dizzying spirals of pleasure shooting through her. But it was more than that.

She'd gone beyond mere attraction. It was more than just liking him, more than friendship. It was all those things plus trust and desire, hot and sweet. And she had finally admitted it to herself last night. She loved him. She was absolutely in love!

And after that kiss, and the look on his face, and the feel of his heart pounding next to hers, she was almost certain he felt the same way. She positively floated on wondrous possibilities.

The best part was, she knew she could trust him. After last night, he fully understood what she'd been through, and how terrifying it had all been. He understood and had promised everything would be okay. She believed him.

She couldn't wait to see him today. This was definitely going to be the best Christmas ever.

The sound of a car engine interrupted Nicole's happy thoughts. Who could that be? Maybe it was Corrie back from grocery shopping or maybe it was UPS with the delivery of paints that she'd ordered. Nicole left Missy's stall and walked over to poke her head through the barn door.

Not Corrie. Not UPS. Her stomach hit the floor as she struggled to understand what she was seeing. Why? Why was there a car with 'Duncan Smith Realty' emblazoned across its doors parked up by the main house?

Nicole took off running towards the house. She could hear the conversation carry across the frigid air before she got close enough for them to notice her. No. Please, no!

"Why are you here?" Garrett's voice carried across the yard. "I left a message to reschedule."

"I'd already left the office. I didn't get it," the other man said. "But since I am here, why don't I look around? It won't take long to give you an exact estimate."

"Now's not a good time." Garrett glanced over his shoulder, back into the house.

"I can give you a ballpark," the realtor offered. "How many acres and buildings?"

"Four hundred and eighty acres, more or less, two houses, that barn over there, a couple of machinery sheds, and a thirty by forty heated shop," Garrett said hurriedly. "But you need to go now. I'll send measurements and specific details later."

"Yeah. Okay. I'll need to see the buildings to be accurate anyways."

Nicole heard him quote a number that shocked her. That much? How could Corrie turn that down? And Garrett looked pleased, blast him.

"That's fine. We'll set something up for January. But for now..." Garrett trailed off as he looked up and saw her approaching. He didn't look half as pleased now, the rat.

Nicole ran the last few steps up to the men on the front porch. Fury raged through her. It radiated from her like waves of heat off blacktop in mid-July. How dare he?

"What is going on here?" she demanded. Her belly churned. She couldn't believe what she'd heard, what he'd done.

"Duncan Smith. Realtor." The man extended his hand, smiling broadly, then hesitantly the smile faded and he withdrew his hand as Nicole ignored the gesture, focusing all her wrath on Garrett instead.

"Garrett?" His name sounded like a snarl on her lips. She didn't care.

"Um. Eh… I'll get back to you later then," Smith said, backing up and retreating to his car. He reversed the car, turned around, and drove down the lane as Nicole faced Garrett down.

"Nicole… Let me explain." He opened the kitchen door and gestured for her to come in.

Nicole glared at him for a moment. She had no desire to go inside, but the bitter cold outside forced her hand. She stormed in only as far as the entrance way and spun to confront him again.

"What do you think you're doing?" she raged, her voice rising with each phrase. "Are you trying to sell this farm? It's not even yours to sell!"

"I just wanted an idea of the current value of the farm, so I could have some facts when I talk to them about it…"

"Talk to them about what? Selling? You want to force them to sell?"

"Calm down, Nicole…"

"Calm down?" Her voice rose even higher. "You want me to calm down? You call a realtor in, after everything I told you last night, after all I've been through, and you think I should *calm down*? You said you understood! You said everything would be okay! I thought you cared about me. I thought you… But I guess I was wrong about that. You just want them to sell this place and kick me out. You know how much this place means to me!"

"It wouldn't be right away. You'd have time…"

"I don't want time!" Nicole yelled. "I don't want to move. Period. I like it *here!*"

"Nic…"

"Don't 'Nic' me!" she cried, tears starting to slip from her eyes. "How long have you been planning this? The whole time? While I'm pouring my heart out to you and you say *nothing*? Just let me spill my guts and pretend to *care*? I told you *everything* and you said *nothing*."

A pain like she'd never known stabbed through her heart. She'd trusted him. Trusted him with her future and trusted him with her heart. He'd betrayed her just like the bandits who'd broken into her house. Worse. This betrayal struck even deeper, because she hadn't loved the thieves, but she had loved Garrett. She'd loved him so much, and he'd played her like a fool. The knowledge was bitter in her mouth.

"I wanted to talk to you about this, but the timing just wasn't right. I hadn't had a chance yet…"

"You never said a thing!" She cut him off once more.

"He never said a thing about what?" Corrie asked.

Startled, Nicole looked over her shoulder to see the door open, with Corrie standing there, and Dawson a step behind her. Corrie looked worried, but Dawson looked furious. Nicole looked back at Garrett and saw his face pale visibly. *Oh yes. You should be afraid, you rat.*

"Garrett had a realtor here," Nicole announced. "He's trying to sell your farm out from under you!"

"GARRETT ANDREW PINE," Corrie said in that way only an angry mother can.

"Hold up!" Garrett raised his hands as if surrendering. "I

was just getting an estimate, so we could discuss real numbers, so…"

"There is nothing to discuss," Corrie stated firmly. "This is my home. I'm not ready to leave."

"Well, isn't this just like you, Super-G," Dawson sneered. "Always thinking you're smarter than everyone else. Always trying to boss everyone around because you know *everything*, right?" He stepped right up and into Garrett's face as he spoke.

Garrett met him eye to eye. "It's not like that. This place is a ton of work and…"

"What do you care?" Dawson demanded. "It's not like you're ever here to help out."

"Come on! I grew up here. I helped plenty over the years. Nicole? Help me out here," Garrett pleaded.

"Oh, no. You lied to me. For weeks! You led me on, thinking your agenda was off the table. You let me believe you cared about us, about me, and all the while you're planning this? How *dare* you. This is Corrie and Abram's house. If it's too much for you to handle, why don't *you* leave?"

"Nicole…" Garrett began.

"NO! Don't even talk to me. To think I trusted you. After everything that happened, I finally trusted someone. You! But you're nothing but a liar. You're worse than the burglars. At least they didn't pretend to care about me! Don't ever speak to me again." With a sob, Nicole spun on her heel, pushed past Corrie still standing in the open door, and bolted down the lane to her house.

CHAPTER TWENTY

G arrett watched her run down the lane, a sick feeling pooling in the pit of his stomach. What had he done? The look on her face had gutted him. The angry words had sliced him open. He'd really blown it this time. Again.

He turned back to face the angry glares of his mother and brother. Dawson was still up in his face, his nose mere inches from Garrett's.

"What?" Garrett snarled. "I was just getting some information so we could have a reasonable discussion as a family. Back off!"

Dawson tensed and clenched his fist. Garrett leaned in a little closer, meeting Dawson's glare with his own. He stared his brother down until the younger man took one step back. Relieved, Garrett also took one step back. He was pretty sure Dawson could take him if it came to a fight, something that hadn't happened since they'd both been kids. Fortunately,

Dawson didn't seem to realize that he was now the bigger and stronger of the two of them.

"That's enough, you two. Honestly, you'd think you weren't grown men the way you're acting. Your father would be ashamed.

"Garrett," she continued, using her firmest 'mom' tone. "You should have talked to me first, not gone behind my back."

"I tried to, remember? But you wouldn't listen."

"That's because I'm not interested in selling. That should have told you all you needed to know."

"Way to mess up, Super-G," Dawson sneered.

"*Don't* call me that. I was trying to help. I was trying to come up with a safer, easier life for Mom and Dad now that Dad has had a stroke. Farming is hard work and you both know it."

"Just because you hate farming doesn't mean we do. Since you hate it so much, why don't you just go on back to the city and leave the farming to those of us who like it. We don't need you!" Dawson asserted from across the kitchen.

"Fine! I'll get my bag and I'll be gone." Garrett turned away, left the kitchen, and headed up the stairs, taking them two at a time.

"Garrett!" his mother called from downstairs.

Every time. Every time he tried to help, this is the thanks he got. Why bother? He grabbed his things and shoved them into his suitcase creating such a jumbled mess he could barely get it closed. It only took a matter of minutes to collect his things and he was heading back down the stairs towards the front door.

"Garrett," Corrie tried again. "Just calm down. Don't leave like this. It's almost Christmas. It's been years since you've been home to spend it with us."

"So what? Everyone's jumping down my throat - just for getting information. I don't know why I even bother trying. Now you know why I usually spend Christmas volunteering overseas - because you all seem happier without me. But if you think you two can manage this farm with Dad incapacitated, have at it! I'm done trying to help."

"Don't pretend you're any help around here!" Dawson shouted as Garrett opened the closet to get his coat.

He shoved his arms into the sleeves, shoved his gloves into his pocket, and shoved his feet into his boots, then stood up, grabbed his bag and reached for the door.

"Garrt."

The word was slurred, but he recognized his father's voice. Garrett looked up to see Abram standing in the hallway, leaning on his cane, watching Garrett with such sorrow on his face. Garrett paused a moment to look at the man he loved so much. He struggled to remember the strong confident farmer and rancher his father had been when Garrett was still a kid, but all he could see was a limp arm missing its hand. All because of him. The guilt crushed down on him like a one-ton hay bale.

And now they all had another reason to hate him. He just couldn't seem to win with his family. He bowed his head. What was the use?

"Gaarrt," his father repeated, still staring earnestly at him.

"I'm sorry, Dad," Garrett said, then stepped through the door, and closed it behind him.

NICOLE DRAPED herself across the top of the box stall wall, staring morosely at Missy as the goat chewed her cud, eyes content and half closed. Nicole had taken her time feeding and checking on the animals. It helped to distract her from the ache in her heart, but only a little.

How could losing something you never really had hurt so much? Sure, she and Garrett had hung out a bit this past month. He'd helped her decorate and taken her to the Christmas party at work. The Christmas Experience had been fun, too, but it wasn't as if they'd been officially dating.

But she had hoped. Hoped with all her heart.

She'd allowed herself to imagine a future with him in it. She'd even envisioned them living together, here, on the farm, maybe helping his folks out together.

What a fool she was. He'd told her he wanted his folks to sell. He'd never said he'd changed his mind about that, but it seemed so long ago. So much had happened since those first days, and she'd just assumed that once he understood all she'd been through he would care enough to change his agenda.

Wrong! He obviously only cared about himself and what he wanted, which was ironic considering his whole righteous position was that he wanted to look after his parents. News flash, buddy. When you're really helping people, it makes them happy, not sad, angry or frustrated. For an otherwise smart guy, he sure wasn't too bright.

She was better off without him. Definitely. She needed a country boy, someone who'd be happy to stay out in the country with her, maybe someone like Garrett's brother,

Dawson. He was handsome too, in a rugged sort of way, and he loved ranching.

Nicole thought about Dawson, his slightly crooked smile and sandy mop of hair. Yes, he was good-looking and charming in his own way, but it felt wrong, somehow. There was no spark when she thought of him, no tingle in her toes or catch in her breath. It was nothing like the rush she felt just looking at Garrett, let alone how she felt being close to him.

In fact, there'd never been anyone who'd made her feel anything even close to how Garrett made her feel. The deep ache in her chest confirmed it. She loved him. She'd fallen hard, allowed herself to trust him, and he'd betrayed her trust and broken her heart. So much for a merry Christmas. Her eyes began to swim with tears, waiting to splash down her cheeks.

A beam of sunlight sliced abruptly through the gloom of the barn as the door opened. Nicole caught her breath in a surge of hope, but quickly released it in a long sigh when she saw Corrie come in and close the door behind her. Of course, it wasn't him, come to apologize.

Nicole blinked quickly and wiped the tears off her face before Corrie could see. She turned her attention back to Missy as Corrie came up beside her.

"How you holding up, Hon?" Corrie asked softly, using her concerned mother tone.

"Okay, I guess. I'm just…so disappointed." Nicole tried to blink back a fresh wave of moisture.

"He meant well, you know. He just gets a little stubborn once he gets an idea in his head."

"I noticed," Nicole replied darkly. "He says he wants to

help, but then he doesn't listen when people tell him what they need, or if he does, he doesn't believe them."

"Well, some people seem to be like that. They decide they know best instead of listening," Corrie agreed.

They both stared at the goat in silence for a while.

"I wish I knew when this goat was going to have her baby," Nicole said.

"Not today, but soon," Corrie replied.

"How do you know?" Nicole had been examining this goat daily and could see no obvious change in her.

"Well, look at her back. Her sides have sunk down, and her hips are protruding. That means the kid has dropped. She could start labor any time between now and five days from now. Looks like her udder is starting to fill, too, so it'll be soon. However, she's eating and looks way too comfortable to be in labor so it won't be today."

"Thanks," Nicole said. "I'm so worried about her. It's cold in this barn."

"She'll be okay," Corrie reassured her. "You've lots of straw for her to snuggle into with her baby, and she's out of the wind. They'll be fine."

"How can you be so sure?"

"Can't," Corrie stated. "Nicole, honey, you can't be sure of anything in this life. Life's not fair, and it's often not predictable. All you can do is use your brain, do your best, and trust the Lord to see you through the rest."

"I guess," Nicole allowed.

"Now the reason I came looking for you is to make sure you're still coming for dinner Christmas Day. I was planning on having everyone there, and it'd be a real shame if you didn't come," Corrie said.

"I'm not sure if I should. Will Garrett be there?" That would just be too awkward and painful to endure.

"I don't know. I haven't spoken to him since he stormed out two days ago. He's not answering his phone," Corrie admitted. "Does it matter?"

"Sort of…"

"You love him, don't you?"

Nicole nodded silently as a single tear streaked her cheek. "But he obviously doesn't love me, or he wouldn't still be trying to get you to sell this farm. He knows it's the only place I feel safe."

"Why is that, Hon?"

"It all goes back to why I was in such a rush to move in here in the first place," Nicole started. She told Corrie about the break-in, the fear she had been living with ever since, and her suspicions about her colleagues.

"Oh, my! That sounds terrifying. Now I understand why you called the police that first week when you were here. Garrett must have scared you half to death." She chuckled a little at that.

"But now you see? I need to be here, where I'm safe. And Garrett knew that, and he didn't care!"

"Oh Honey, I'm sure Garrett does care. He just knows that farm life isn't any safer than city life."

"What do you mean?" Nicole didn't like the sound of that.

"I know you feel safer out here but living in the country doesn't mean you're immune to crime," Corrie said. "Rural crime is an increasing problem. Usually, it's folks trying to steal toys like quads or snowmobiles, but occasionally there are violent confrontations."

"I didn't know that," Nicole admitted quietly. She had felt so much safer here, and now hearing Corrie say it wasn't true was unsettling. She tried to push back the thread of anxiety curling in her stomach. It couldn't be worse here than in the city. It just couldn't. "What can I do?"

"Well, like I said before, be smart, do your best, and trust God for the rest. Everything works out the way it's meant to." Corrie gave Nicole a big bear hug. "Now don't you worry. It's Christmas, and we're going to have peace and joy in spite of it all. You'll see. And I'm counting on you being there for Christmas. I want you to meet my daughter, Jess. Dawson will be picking her up from the airport tomorrow afternoon, just in time for Christmas Eve. Garrett was supposed to do it, but… Well. You know."

"Thank you, Corrie. I'll be there. What time?"

"Three o'clock or so. That way you'll be in time for the appetizers and homemade eggnog."

"All right. See you then."

Nicole watched Corrie leave the barn and head back outside. She'd go to dinner, simply because the older woman was so kind. It was the least she could do, but as for peace and joy, Nicole doubted she would be feeling much of that for a very long time.

CHAPTER TWENTY-ONE

*G*arrett slumped in his armchair, sipping a drink, and staring out his apartment window. Outside, numerous balconies had Christmas lights strung along their railings, and some industrious person had even decorated the boom of a construction crane. Garrett's balcony, however, was bare, as was the inside of his apartment. Having not been home for Christmas in years, he didn't own any decorations, so had nothing to put out, even if he felt inclined to do so, which he didn't.

His apartment had never felt emptier, or lonelier. He should probably go to work, pretend to be useful, but he couldn't summon the energy. All he could do was slouch on the sofa and think about Nicole and the gaping hole in his heart with her gone.

The big cold apartment felt so empty compared to his parents' house, or even the little house Nicole rented. Why had he thought living in the city was better? He couldn't recall now. He only knew he missed her. He missed her so much, the thought of moving back to the country didn't sound so bad after all.

"*It's the most wonderful time of the year,*" sang some overly perky woman on the radio. Bah! Garrett slouched deeper in his seat.

His phone rang, vibrating across the end table until he grabbed it and glanced at the number. Surprisingly, it wasn't his mother again. He had been ignoring her calls for two days now. No, it was the college calling. Mild curiosity being better than remembering all the ways he'd messed up, he decided to answer the call.

"Hello?"

"Hello? Dr. Pine? This is Mavis, from the College Art Department."

"Yes?"

"I just wanted to let you know that the two paintings you purchased still haven't been picked up. With it being only two days until Christmas, I was a little worried. I thought you might want to make other arrangements to collect them. We're only open until noon tomorrow, because it will be Christmas Eve."

"There was a guy, a Tim somebody, who was supposed to pick them up for me," Garrett said with irritation. You just couldn't count on anyone these days.

"Yes. We know. But he hasn't arrived, and we haven't been able to contact him," Mavis replied.

Garrett almost told her to keep them. What did he need with those paintings now? He'd be alone for Christmas and didn't need unwanted gifts sitting around reminding him how he'd blown it again.

And yet...

The paintings were part of Nicole, her creations. He had lost his chance with her, but he could still have that one little part of her. Some small thing to remind him. As if he could ever forget.

"I'll... I'll come get them myself. What time are you open to?"

"Four o'clock today, and from eight until noon tomorrow," Mavis replied. She also sounded too perky.

"Fine. I'll be there. I don't know when." Garrett hung up, belatedly realizing he'd probably been so abrupt as to be rude.

Elvis was now crooning about a blue Christmas. That hit too close to home. Time to go for a drive. Garrett turned off the radio, collected his coat, and headed down the hall to the elevator.

He made his way down to the parking garage, opened the back hatch to flatten out the seats to make room for the paintings, and then stood there, dumbfounded. The back of his SUV was piled with presents for the family they'd agreed to sponsor. He'd completely forgotten!

They weren't even wrapped yet. He ran his hand through his hair and groaned. Could this Christmas get any worse?

So now he had to pick up the paintings this afternoon, wrap the gifts tonight, which meant stopping for gift wrap, tape and bows, and then tomorrow morning pick up the food hamper from the church and deliver all of it before he could come back to a quiet, miserable, empty house. Great.

He hadn't wanted to go back north at all. Now he was stuck. Hopefully, he wouldn't run into Nicole at the church. He just couldn't face her right now. Maybe ever.

It took three trips around the block before Garrett realized the address he was looking for was probably in the trailer park. He turned into the main gate, and slowly wove his way through the single lane maze of trailers until he found the right one. He parked his SUV, then glanced back at the pile of things behind him. This would have been fun if Nicole were here to help deliver the gifts, but without her…

Garrett sighed deeply and got out of his vehicle. Hopefully, the dad would help him carry the stuff in. He walked up to the door, and knocked.

"Hello?" The door opened to reveal a man not much older than Garrett, with sandy-colored hair and a warm smile.

"Hi. Merry Christmas. My name is Garrett. I'm here from Home Church with your hamper."

"Oh! Thank you."

"It's just in the car, if you wouldn't mind," Garrett started to say.

"Helping? Absolutely," the young dad finished. "My name is Paul. Thank you so much for doing this. My girls will be so happy." Paul offered his hand to Garrett.

Garrett shook his hand. It was a good solid handshake. Paul seemed warm and friendly. He turned and led the way back to his SUV.

Paul grabbed the enormous box of food, while Garrett took several bags stuffed with gifts, and followed Paul back into his house. Inside was neat and clean, if a little sparse. There was one old couch and a coffee table in the sitting area, and what looked like a table from a patio set with three chairs and a well-worn high chair in the kitchen. Red felt Christmas stockings had been pinned up along the couch, a spot likely picked due to the lack of a fireplace.

"Can you put all the gifts in here?" Paul asked, indicating the hall closet which was mostly empty.

Garrett started stashing gifts in the closet.

Paul began unloading the food into his refrigerator and cupboards. "I really appreciate this help. My wife would be so grateful that the kids won't miss out on Christmas."

"Do you mind me asking where she is?" Garrett asked.

"She had breast cancer," Paul replied quietly.

"I am so sorry," Garrett offered. "I didn't mean to pry."

"It's all right. When Allison got sick, I quit my job to look after her and the girls. When the employment insurance ran out, we used up our savings. By the time she passed, we had to downsize. I picked this trailer because the trailer park is clean and we have nice big windows that are hard to find in a basement suite. I look after the girls during the day, and drive cab in the evenings while the neighbor babysits for me. We're doing okay, but there isn't a lot left over for extras, like Christmas presents."

"That's tough. I'm glad we can help out with the kids," Garrett said.

"Yes. They're going to be thrilled, but we have to hurry. The girls are due back from their play date with the neighbors in a little while. I want this all hidden away until tomorrow morning," Paul said, grinning ear to ear.

"I get it. The old 'Santa came last night' magic," Garrett agreed.

Paul chuckled. "Not exactly. More like 'look what God has provided' magic."

"But this is all just from people, from the church," Garrett reminded him. God wasn't a magic genie that zapped things into existence.

"Of course. But it's God who places the love in their hearts to sacrifice for others, to provide food and gifts for strangers who'd go without otherwise. Isn't that why you're here? You don't even know us, but you've taken time from your Christmas Eve morning to bring all this here, to make Christmas special," Paul said earnestly.

Garrett felt his face warm. Was that really why he was here? Just from a place of love for others? His conscience poked him. That wasn't it, was it? There was another reason. The same reason he did all his charity work.

Paul studied his face intently. "Why *are* you here?" he asked astutely.

Garrett cleared his throat uncomfortably. "I, uh... I guess I'm trying to make up for past mistakes. For the times I wasn't there when I should have been."

"I see. What have you done so far? To make up for it?" Paul asked, sitting backwards on a kitchen chair and leaning towards Garrett with obvious interest.

"Well... Every year since I graduated Med school, I go to Mexico for a couple of months with Doctors Without Borders to provide medical care to poor villages. And when I'm here in Canada, I donate to charity and volunteer where I can. I just try to help people."

"How long have you been doing this?" Paul asked.

"Six years, I guess. Why?"

"Wow. You must have done a lot of bad things, huh?" Paul prodded. He propped his elbow on the chair back and rested his chin on his palm, looking as if he expected a detailed story.

"No. Not that many. It's a long story, but... It's just the one thing." Garrett scowled. *Sheesh, buddy. What are you implying? I'm not a monster.*

"So it must have been *really* bad, huh? Did you murder someone?" Paul dropped his hand and leaned even farther forward.

"What? No! I didn't murder anyone. It was a mistake, I mean I wasn't even there, but..." Garrett trailed off, feeling helpless. *What was with this guy?*

"If you weren't there, then how could it be your fault?" Paul asked.

Garrett turned away and ran his hand through his hair. It was no one's business, yet he found himself wanting to explain about the accident, and the guilt that followed him constantly. So, he did. Paul listened quietly as he told his story.

"And so you go every year to help?"

"Yes. And now my dad has had a stroke, and I'm trying to help him and Mom out, but they're fighting everything I'm trying to do for them."

"Hmm." Paul looked thoughtful a moment, then looked Garrett straight in the eye and asked, "When will you be done?"

"What do you mean? Done what?" Garrett asked.

"When will all this free help you give have made up for your mistake? I mean, what you're doing is wonderful, but when will it all be enough?"

"I…I don't know." He'd never thought that far through it. How much was enough? When would the scales be even?

Paul leaned back and smiled. "Maybe you don't have to fix everything. Maybe you should just apologize and be forgiven."

Garrett just stared at Paul as if he'd grown another head. It couldn't be that simple. Could it?

"Apologize?"

"Yes. Apologize. To God first, and then to the people you've wronged. Then you can still do all those same good things, but you'll do them *because* you're forgiven, not because you're trying to *earn* your forgiveness."

Garrett felt stunned. Just apologize? Could that really be all that was needed?

"You think they'll actually forgive me if I ask?" Garrett wondered aloud.

"Yes. I think they will," Paul responded. "It is Christmas, after all."

"Christmas is about love, not forgiveness," Garrett said.

"But you're wrong," Paul answered. "Christmas is all about forgiveness. Because God loved us so much, He wanted to forgive all our mistakes, He sent His son Jesus to pay the price for them, so we could all be forgiven."

"I never thought of it that way before," Garrett admitted. "But you're right. You're absolutely right."

Garrett reached his hand out to Paul, who stood and gripped his hand in a firm grasp.

"Thank you," Garrett said, "I came here to help you, but I feel like you've helped me more than I did you."

Paul pulled him into a brief hug. "And thank you, as well, for making my girls' Christmas special. Look! Here they come."

The door opened, and two blond cherubs with pink cheeks and curly hair exploded into the home.

"Look, Daddy! We made gingerbread cookies," the oldest announced. She held out a paper plate holding a pile of cookies covered with plastic wrap.

The youngest just threw herself at her now crouching father, almost knocking him over. She snuggled up to her dad then peered up shyly towards Garrett.

"Hello." Garrett smiled down at her.

She hid her face in her dad's shirt.

Her elder sister held out the plate towards him and asked, "Would you like a cookie?"

He could tell from her expression that she was hoping he wouldn't want one, so he said, "They look delicious, but I'm so full from breakfast, I don't have any room left. You'd better eat one for me."

"Okay," she said happily, bouncing over to the counter to put down the plate.

Garrett said goodbye to Paul and his girls and went back to his car. It was past noon, he was hungry, and he wanted to get home.

$\mathcal{I}$t was Christmas Eve and Nicole sprawled on her couch, listening to Rudolph the Redneck Reindeer twang out of the radio. Bah, humbug. She sighed deeply.

Her pretty tree sat alone in her living room, its lights twinkling off and on repeatedly. The UPS box from her parents in Arizona sat on the floor in the corner, unopened. She knew there'd be brightly wrapped gifts from them inside, but she just didn't have the heart to place them under her tree. She didn't have the heart for anything.

Upstairs, in her art room, the painting she'd done for Abram and Corrie sat on its easel with a big red bow on the corner. The one she'd been painting for Garrett sat unfinished in its spot. To be sure, it was mostly done, but there were still some finishing touches needed. She just couldn't bring herself to complete it.

The same applied to her Christmas baking. Nothing had been done this week as originally planned. She'd just moped around like a slug. Oh, well. At least she wouldn't gain another five pounds this year.

Nicole dragged herself off the couch and wandered over to the window. She stood there, looking out over the frozen ground, hugging herself, lost in thought. Was it only a few days ago she'd thought this was going to be her best Christmas ever? Now it was all ruined.

Well, it was long past time to do her animal chores. She was really late today, and the goats knew it. She could hear Norbert complaining loudly about not having his breakfast yet and it was almost noon. Good ol' Norby. At least he missed her, if only because she brought the food.

Nicole bundled up in her winter gear of boots, parka, touque, snow pants, and gloves, and then headed out to the yard. The air stung her cheeks, and inside her nose, the little hairs froze and melted again every time she inhaled and exhaled.

Her routine was to first carry two large buckets of water from the house out to Norbert's pen to top off his heated bucket, and then to top off the chicken coop water. Of course, the lady goats had their own automatic heated water station. She would open the small chicken door to the coop, so the hens could go out to their heated water bowl for a drink, then top up their food dispenser inside the coop where a heat lamp kept things at a warmer level of cold.

After the hens were done, she carried hay out to the goats, dragging the bale in a bright orange calf sled, first to Norby, and then to the girls. After all the outside creatures were cared for, she had some time to hang out in the barn, fussing over Missy, and feeding the lame cow who was now almost well enough to rejoin the rest of her herd outside. Nicole suspected they were allowing her to remain in the barn just to keep Missy company, and because a large cow generates a fair deal of heat and was helping to keep the small barn warmer.

Nicole had just stepped inside and closed the barn door when she heard a car engine come up the drive. Must be Dawson with Jess. Nicole was curious but resisted taking a peek. She would get to meet Jess tomorrow. For now, they'd want some family time to catch up.

Nicole had been puttering in the barn about fifteen minutes when she became aware of yelling outside. Was that Garrett fighting with Dawson, again? But no... that was Corrie's voice, and a man.

A chill ran up Nicole's spine. That voice! That same voice. She recognized it from the break-in at her old place. She whimpered as fear sliced through her. She cringed back against the barn wall paralyzed with fear. What should she do? Her phone was sitting on the kitchen table, in her house. She hadn't thought she'd need it to do her chores.

Corrie was yelling again, but Nicole couldn't hear what was being said. Heart hammering through her chest, she crept up to the barn door and cracked it open. In a cold sweat she peered out with one eye. The voices became clearer.

"Get out of Nicole's house right now!" Corrie demanded. She was standing back from Nicole's back porch, yelling at a man standing in her doorway.

"I told you, lady. She's a friend of mine. She said I could go in and get my stuff," the guy snapped back.

"Nicole said no such thing. If she had, she'd be here to

hand it to you instead of you tearing her place apart. You get out of there!" Corrie yelled back.

"She must have forgot I was coming," the guy asserted.

That voice. Where else had she heard it? Hiding behind the door, shaking like a leaf, it was hard to think straight. She knew that voice. Where? Then it hit her. It was Tim! That Tim kid who'd been so persistent at the Christmas party. Tim, what's his name? Cardston.

He stood blocking the back porch entrance to her mudroom, the door she hadn't bothered to lock when she went outside because she was just going to the barn. Corrie stood back about ten feet. From what Nicole could see from behind her, she had her feet planted and was ready for a fight.

"Then you can just wait for her to get back instead of rummaging through her house!"

"I need it now and I ain't waiting no more. Just give me my key and I'll go, but I ain't leaving without it, old lady!"

Nicole gritted her teeth. Anger pushed back against the terror coursing through her. How dare he speak to Corrie that way? And what was that about a key? Nicole vaguely remembered a key. Where'd she put it? It seemed so long ago. Think, Nicole!

"You leave right this minute or I'm calling the police," Corrie threatened. She pulled out her phone and started tapping the screen.

"Oh no you don't!" Tim leapt forward, snatching the phone from Corrie's hand before she could react. He flung it away, behind him, and grabbed Corrie by the front of her jacket. Hauling her up close, he snarled into her face, "Gimme my KEY!"

Corrie! Panic surged through Nicole. She had to do something. What if he hurt Corrie? What if he hit her, like he had Nicole? She couldn't hide here like a coward while Corrie was in danger.

"Go to hell," Corrie said defiantly.

Tim raised a fist as if to hit her. Adrenaline surged through Nicole. She had to act fast. She had to do something, but what?

Oh, Jesus, help me!

GARRETT DROVE south out of Red Deer, hitting the highway back towards Calgary. He should go home. He should. He'd messed everything up with his family, and even worse with Nicole. There was no point in trying to make it right. He'd tried that before, and it never worked...But Paul's advice wouldn't stop rolling through his head.

Just apologize. Had he ever tried that? It seemed so simple, so obvious, that he must have done that... But had he?

He thought back. Sure, he'd tried to make up for it, but had he ever just humbled himself and apologized? After some thought he realized his giant ego hadn't allowed him to do that.

He felt the strongest urge to go straight to his parents' farm then and there. He hesitated. That would be dumb. They were still mad at him, he was sure of it. Maybe he should just let them all calm down for a few days, wait until after Christmas. Spending Christmas alone was bound to be better than an awkward, strained Christmas tiptoeing around everyone's hurt feelings. Maybe they'd even miss him and be more inclined to accept his apology.

The turnoff for his parents' place was fast approaching. He felt the urge again but pushed it down. Later. He'd do it later. Right now, he didn't feel like it.

He drove past the turnoff. The urge hit him again, stronger. Why couldn't he drop this?

Then it hit him. He remembered! The last time he'd ignored an urge like this, his father had lost a hand. He was doing it again, making that same mistake!

With a sudden sense of urgency, Garrett knew something was happening, something bad, and whatever it was, he needed to be there. He'd already missed his exit, so he'd have to take the next one and circle back. Would he be in time? He prayed so.

CHAPTER TWENTY-THREE

*R*age swelled within Nicole, pushing the fear aside, and giving her strength she hadn't guessed she had. How dare that little punk lay his hands on Corrie? She seethed, watching through the crack of the barn door. She had to do something, but what? Think, Nicole, think!

What did she have as a weapon? She looked frantically around the barn. Tin pails, a rubber bucket, a pitchfork. That might work.

Nicole grabbed the pitchfork. Screwing up her courage she burst through the barn door as Tim started shaking Corrie.

"You leave her alone!" Nicole screamed at him as she ran towards them, pitchfork extended in front of her.

Tim swore profusely. "Why do you always gotta show up when you're supposed to be gone somewhere else?" He shoved Corrie backwards into a large pile of snow that had been blown against the side of the covered porch, and turned to face Nicole. "Now I'm going to have to deal with you so you don't tell the cops."

"Stay back!" Nicole yelled at him, waving her pitchfork at him. "Corrie? Corrie, are you all right?"

"Oof! I... I think so. But I'm stuck." She flailed her arms from the deep snowbank, trying to turn over or find leverage to get up again.

"Gimme that!" Tim swung his arm towards Nicole while she was distracted, knocking the pitchfork aside enough to grab the handle and yank it from her grasp.

Nicole yelped and jumped back as Tim lunged for her. Rage infused his face. He flung the pitchfork behind him, sending it spinning like a frisbee across the yard. Nicole spun on the spot and ran, making it as far as Norbert's pen before he caught up with her. She unlatched the gate and flung it open, but Tim grabbed the hood of her parka and wrenched her back before she could get away.

He grabbed her arm and spun her around to face him. Holding her by both arms now, he shook her, yelling into her face, "Why aren't you in Arizona? You always go to Arizona for Christmas." His face was mottled with rage as he yelled from mere inches away.

"What difference does it make? I'm here, not there. Let go! You're hurting me!" Belatedly, she realized she should have run for the house instead of up the lane. She could probably have gotten to her phone long enough to have punched in 911 before Tim caught up to her. Too late now.

"Where's my key? Give it back!" Tim raged in her face.

"What key?" No telling what he'd do to them once he had his stupid key back and didn't need them anymore. She had to stall, buy enough time to figure out what to do. She had no phone, Corrie was stuck in a snowbank, and there was no one to help. Oh, Lord, please send help.

"I left a key behind at your other place. I need it back! They'll kill me if I don't get it back!"

"Stop yelling! Let me think. I think I remember seeing a key somewhere."

"Where?" Tim screamed, shaking her so hard her teeth rattled.

Out of the corner of her eye, Nicole saw movement. A large, hammer-shaped head was approaching from behind Tim. Norbert had left his pen!

"Tell me where it is!" Tim repeated, practically frothing at the mouth.

Behind him, Norbert baa'd loudly and pushed his head into Tim's thigh. Startled, Tim glanced down at the goat who was now staring back at him, a determined expression on his stubborn goat face.

"Get away from me you stupid goat!" Tim dropped one of Nicole's arms and took a swing at Norbert, smacking him squarely in the face with his palm.

"Ow!" Tim yelled, shaking his hand in pain. "Dumb stupid goat!"

Norbert dropped his head, stomped one hoof, and hummed loudly. A plume of steam escaped his nostrils.

Nicole wrenched back, trying to run, but Tim's grip was too strong on her other arm. He yanked her back roughly.

"Hold still!" he snarled. "I said get away, goat!" He swung his fist and punched Norbert in the face with all his might.

A GIANT PLUME of dust trailed Garrett's SUV as he sped down the frozen gravel road towards his parents' farm. He couldn't seem to shake the sense of urgency that had him pushing the speed limit. He barely slowed enough to make the turn up their long driveway, then accelerated up the lane until he slid to a stop in front of Nicole's little house. There was another car there, one he didn't recognize.

His mind took in the scene in a flash. His mother, stuck butt first in a deep snowbank beside Nicole's porch, his father, leaning on his cane, watching from the wrap-around porch of the big house, and some guy manhandling Nicole while she struggled to get away.

And there was Norbert.

Anger like he'd never known surged through him. Garrett leapt from his SUV and ran towards Nicole. It felt like he was barely moving as he watched the drama unfold. As Nicole struggled to get away, the guy swung his fist at Norbert and hit him in the face.

Ooo! Wrong move. Garrett almost felt sorry for him. Almost.

Norbert dropped his head, took a step back, then reared up to his full height on two back legs, and hurled his head full force into the guy's leg. Garrett heard the loud crack as it snapped.

There was a blood-curdling scream as the guy collapsed to the ground, releasing Nicole who had been leaning back as far away from him as she could. She stumbled briefly, then ran straight into Garrett's arms as he rushed to meet her.

He enfolded her, feeling such a flood of relief he almost sobbed. She was safe! Thank you, Jesus!

"Are you okay? Did he hurt you? Nicole?"

"I'm okay. I'm okay," she replied, her voice surprisingly firm. "But your mom. He pushed your mom!"

"Mom? You okay?" Garrett called out to her.

Nicole's attacker was writhing on the ground, clutching his knee, and moaning, while Norbert circled him, humming his displeasure. Garrett and Nicole ran back to where his mother was still flailing her arms, trying in vain to roll herself over in the deep snowdrift.

"Garrett. Give me a hand here. I feel like a stupid turtle stuck on its back," she said, puffing with all the effort she'd exerted.

Garrett and Nicole each grabbed a hand and carefully pulled her out of the snow and back onto her feet.

"That's better," she said, dusting the snow off her pants. "How'd you get that jerk? I couldn't see what was happening."

"We didn't get him," Nicole said with an evil smile. "Norbert did."

"Ooo!" His mom winced. "That explains the screaming then."

"Are you hurt, Mom?" Garrett asked. If that jerk had hurt her…

"Just my pride, son. I'll be fine otherwise."

"I hear sirens," Nicole said, looking up and back down the lane towards the road.

"Me too," Garrett agreed. He could see lights approaching in the distance. "Who called the cops?"

"I didn't. That jerk took my phone and pitched it. He better not have broken it," his mom replied, scowling, as she started a search of the nearby ground where it might have landed.

"I left mine in the house," Nicole said, shrugging her shoulders.

"I didn't have time to call either," Garrett said, puzzled. "So who?"

"ME!" Abram called out, waving his cane on the porch.

Well, what do you know? Garrett found himself grinning. The old guy wasn't completely helpless after all. Taking Nicole's hand in his, the two of them walked back towards the intruder curled on the ground as the sirens grew steadily closer. Norbert poked him roughly with his nose.

Sobbing and whimpering, the guy begged, "Get it away. Get it away from me."

"I think I know this guy," Garrett said, staring down at him now that he was finally able to get a good look. "Isn't that...?"

"Tim. From the Christmas party," Nicole supplied, grimly. "Turns out he was one of the guys who broke into my basement suite."

Oh no! With a sinking feeling, the realization hit him. He'd been the one to give Tim Nicole's new address. He'd done it again! She'd never forgive him for this one. Never in a million years.

"Found it!" his mom called out, waving her phone for them to see. "Now I'll go get a cupful of grain to lure Norby back into his pen. He'd follow you through the gates of Hell for a cup of grain," she said with a chuckle.

"I'll do it, Corrie," Nicole offered. "You should rest."

"Bah! I'm fine. Besides, the cops are here already, and

they'll want to talk to you. Go on now. I've got it." She patted Nicole's shoulder, then hurried off towards the barn for the needed cup of grain.

Norbert raised his head from harassing Tim and glowered at the rest of them. He snorted and waved his horns menacingly. Garrett took a cautious step back, motioning for the cops who were approaching to do the same.

The rest of the afternoon was a blur.

IN THE ENSUING chaos of police, ambulance, goats, victims and bystanders, Nicole felt like she was in the center of a hurricane, the calm in the center of the storm. Her heart still raced with the adrenaline rush; she could feel the pulse in her throat and the hammering in her chest but she felt none of the crippling fear like before. This was exhilarating, like the moment before jumping off a bridge into a deep river below.

Three police cars had arrived, sirens blaring, and stopped strategically surrounding the four of them. Constable Wilson was there again, with two other officers. He pulled Nicole aside as one officer checked Tim out and the other pulled Corrie aside to talk by Norbert's pen. Nicole caught Garrett's eye briefly, but he turned away as soon as he noticed her and headed up towards the main house. What was that look in his eyes? Regret? He wasn't happy, that was for sure.

Nicole's heart dropped. When he'd first arrived and sprinted to rescue her after Norbert had smashed into Tim like the Hulk, she'd been sure he was happy to see her. She'd felt so safe and loved, crushed tightly to his chest. His heart had been hammering into her ear. His voice, when he'd asked if she was hurt, had held such concern. She'd felt sure he would apologize for the realtor thing, and maybe they could work things out. She loved him so much!

But no. As soon as the police arrived, Garrett pulled away and now he wouldn't even look at her. Maybe he wasn't sorry at all. Maybe he figured she'd be anxious to leave here, too, after this incident, and that would play right into his agenda of selling off the farm.

Well, fat chance, buddy. She had no intention of leaving because, as crazy as it sounded, she wasn't afraid anymore. That surprised her. She didn't understand why.

"I need to ask some questions." Constable Wilson interrupted her thoughts. "Can we take this inside?"

"Yes. Of course," Nicole replied. As the adrenaline wore off, the pervading cold seeped through the thick layers of her clothing. She felt a shiver run up her spine.

Nicole and Wilson retreated towards her back door. Nicole led the way in through the mud room but stopped abruptly at the threshold of her kitchen. Cupboards were flung open, drawers had been pulled out and their contents strewn on the floor, even the fridge door stood ajar.

"What the...!" Nicole put both hands to her head, staring around the room in disbelief at the mess. No wonder Corrie had been yelling at him.

"Do you have any idea what he was looking for?" Wilson asked. "Don't touch anything." He pulled out a camera and snapped some pictures.

"He kept screeching about a key." Nicole went back into

the mud room to strip off her outerwear. The house was very warm compared to outside.

"Do you know what key he's referring to?" Wilson undid his winter coat, revealing the soft armor underneath. He prowled carefully through the mess, looking things over and taking pictures.

"I sort of remember a key, but he had me so upset I couldn't recall where I'd seen it. Let me think." Nicole frowned in concentration, chewing absently on her thumbnail for a few moments. "Oh! I think I know."

She rushed into her living room, followed by Wilson. A drawer from the end table had been dumped out, the cushions from the couch tossed about, and the books pulled off the shelves and thrown on the floor, but fortunately her pretty Christmas tree had been spared destruction. It still sat in the corner, lights twinkling hopefully, waiting for Christmas to arrive.

Nicole tiptoed through the debris to her very tall bookshelf, reached way up, and felt around on top. There! There it was, right where she'd left it that first week. "Found it!

"Here." She handed the key over to Constable Wilson. "I found it when I was unpacking, and then forgot all about it. I have no idea what it belongs to, but I know it's not mine. Maybe this is what he was looking for."

Wilson looked the key over carefully. "This might be for a bus locker or maybe a self-storage. We'll figure it out."

They moved back into the kitchen for the inevitable questions. Nicole made tea and answered as best she could with what she knew. Outside her kitchen window, Nicole could see Norbert standing on his hind legs, front feet propped on the fence, leaning over the rail towards Tim who still lay on the ground. An ambulance was finally pulling into the yard.

Wilson put his notepad away and stood up. "I think that's all for now, Ms. Mitro, but we may have more questions for you later. We'll be in touch. You'll probably have to testify later if this goes to trial, but that won't be for a while yet." He moved to the door and turned back just before leaving. "I hope you have a Merry Christmas, Ms. Mitro."

"Thank you. Merry Christmas to you, too." Nicole threw her coat back on and followed him outside.

She wandered over to where Corrie stood by the fence. She glanced at Tim, moaning on the ambulance stretcher as the attendants strapped him down. One hand was handcuffed to the stretcher, a slight overkill since the boy wouldn't be going anywhere on that leg for a while. Served him right.

Still leaning over the fence, Norbert baa'd loudly and waved his horns, looking for a more worthy opponent.

"Keep it away!" Tim screeched pitifully, cringing back on his stretcher.

"Hold still," one attendant urged without sympathy while the two of them hefted the stretcher up into the back of the ambulance.

Norbert snorted a large plume of steam from his nostrils. "Good boy, Norby," Nicole said, and gave him a little scratch under the chin. "Bonus grain for you tonight, old man."

Who'd have thought Norby would be her secret weapon? Nicole watched the ambulance pull away. Tim had terrorized her in her basement suite and left her fearful for months. Now he'd tried to terrorize her here, too, but she'd fought back, and she'd won, though she hadn't done it alone.

"You really okay?" Nicole asked Corrie.

"I'm fine, Honey. I'm just glad it's all over now." Corrie smiled and opened her arms wide.

Nicole slid in for one of Corrie's bear hugs. It felt warm, and safe, and wonderful. The only thing that could be better, was if the hug came from Garrett, but he had disappeared up to the house. Nicole assumed one of the officers was still in there talking with Garrett and Abram, since it was only Wilson and one other man conferring together by their cars outside.

"I'd better go check on my husband," Corrie said as she pulled away.

"Yes. I have a huge mess to clean up, too." Nicole sighed. "Thank you. So much. For everything."

"Any time, Hon. I'll come back later to help you clean up."

"Please don't worry about it. I'll be fine," Nicole said. In truth, she needed time to think. Everything had happened so fast. She was still trying to make sense of it all.

"If you insist, but I still expect you for supper tomorrow. Merry Christmas." Corrie turned and began walking up the lane towards the main house.

"Merry Christmas," Nicole offered before retreating back to the shambles of her kitchen.

Inside once more, she surveyed the mess and sighed. So much for her safe haven. Corrie had been right. Crime could follow you anywhere. Maybe it really didn't matter if she stayed here or went back to her old life in the city. If Garrett wanted her gone, was there any reason to stay here, or to even see him again? The heartbreaking truth was, no, there wasn't.

One thing was for sure. Christmas dinner at Corrie's tomorrow would be a hard pass if Garrett's SUV was still here by then. It might be best to call up a friend and invite herself over to Christmas dinner somewhere else.

CHAPTER TWENTY-FOUR

*G*arrett closed the door behind the police officer and turned back to face his parents who were sitting at the kitchen table, watching him intently. He knew why. Just before the officer left, he'd confided about how Tim Cardston had gotten Nicole's new address. From him. He wasn't happy about it.

He could imagine what they were thinking. 'Way to go, Garrett. Screwed up again - same as always.'

"Does anyone want some tea?" he asked. It was a good excuse to stall the inevitable.

"That sounds lovely," his mom said.

"Yesh," his father managed, his voice only a little slurred. He seemed to be improving slowly every day, much to Garrett's relief.

Garrett made the tea, putting cream, sugar and honey on the table. He placed their two cups down on the table before getting his own cup and sitting across from them. He made a point of stirring the honey into his for longer than was actually necessary.

"Well, that was some excitement," his mom ventured.

His father nodded agreement. He took a sip of his tea, his good hand firm and steady.

"Are you sure that guy didn't hurt you, Mom?" Garrett asked.

"I might have bruised my butt, but I'll live," she reassured him.

They all stared at their cups a few minutes until the tension was unbearable. Paul's advice from earlier blared inside Garrett's head like a bullhorn. Just apologize. Had that only been this morning? Time to get it over with. If they wouldn't forgive him, then he wanted to be long gone before Dawson got home with Jess.

Gripping his mug so tight his knuckles turned white, Garrett said, "Look. I… I'm sorry."

"Sorry about what, Honey?" His mom looked intently at him. Her face was soft and kind, with no hint of censure.

Garrett forced himself to meet her gaze. He wanted to be sure they understood. He meant it. "Sorry about today for starters. You heard what I said to the police. It's my fault Tim got this address. I gave it to him. I'm a complete idiot handing out this address to a stranger. You've every right to be furious with me."

"Oh, Garrett. Don't blame yourself. You didn't know he was up to no good. It's not your fault." His mom smiled, warm and reassuring.

"So you forgive me?"

"There's nothing to forgive. You did nothing wrong."

"So, that's a 'yes'?" Garrett persisted.

"Yes, yes, of course," his mother assured him.

"Okay. Good. What about bringing in a realtor. You're right. I wasn't listening to you or what you wanted. I... I'm sorry for that, too. Will you forgive me?"

"Yes, of course, Honey. We love you. We'll always forgive you." His mother reached across the table to give his hand a squeeze. Beside her, his father nodded again.

"Okay." He cleared his throat. "That's the small stuff. What about the big one?"

"What 'big one' are you referring to?" His mom sounded confused; a little crease formed between her eyebrows.

"You know." Garrett dropped his eyes, unable to look at them straight.

"You'll have to explain a bit more," his mother pressed.

"Dad's hand. It's my fault he lost his hand. If I had only been there to help, it never would have happened. It's all my fault." Even he could hear the anguish in his own voice. He paused, held his breath, waited.

"Garrett, don't be foolish. How could it be your fault? You weren't even there when it happened," his mom said firmly.

"But, if I had been there to help, if he hadn't been all alone, it would never have happened. It's my fault for being so lazy."

"First of all," his mother started, "your dad wasn't all alone. Dawson was there helping. Secondly, your father's no child. He's been farming his whole life and he knows the dangers. He knew he was tired. He knew he should have called it a night, but he kept on going, and he made a mistake. That's the truth of it. Thirdly, how dare you call yourself lazy? You're the hardest working young man I know."

Garrett finally looked up at them, wanting desperately to believe it wasn't his fault. Did they mean it? Truly? He looked at each of his parents in turn, both faces earnest, his father nodding agreement.

"Not your fault, boy," his father added. "My own."

"But I was always ditching farm chores. I should have helped more. I thought you were disappointed in me."

"Never," the old man said, shaking his head. "Proud of you."

"You were never lazy," his mother added. "We saw how hard you worked on your grades, studying all the time. We deliberately cut you some slack on the farm work because we knew you had it in you to become a great doctor. We couldn't be more proud of you." His mom smiled reassuringly at him.

"So then...you forgive me?" He still couldn't quite accept it.

"Oh, you silly man! Give your mom a hug." She pushed her chair back to come around and engulfed him in a big bear hug as he stood to meet her. "Have you been dragging around this guilt all this time?"

"Yes," he mumbled into her shoulder.

"Well enough of that. You let all that go. No one blames you because it's not your fault. Got it? Now we're going to have the best Christmas ever!"

Garrett gave her one last squeeze before releasing her. He felt lighter than he could remember in a long time, lighter and freer. He could almost imagine having the best Christmas ever, but there was still a very large cloud hanging over his head. He'd led Tim straight to Nicole. When she found out, he couldn't imagine her forgiving him as easily as his parents had.

While his mother started getting supper ready, and his father settled into his easy chair, Garrett took his tea to the kitchen window, and looked across the yard to the glow in Nicole's kitchen. Maybe he should just go and get it over with?

He had almost made up his mind to go over when two beams of light cut through the almost dark yard. That would be Dawson returning from the airport with his little sister, Jess. His heart lifted. Unlike Dawson, Jess was always happy to see him. He adored her right back. It had been ages since they'd talked, and he couldn't wait to catch up.

Getting dumped by Nicole, though? That could wait.

CHAPTER TWENTY-FIVE

*I*t was nine o'clock before Nicole finished cleaning up the mess in her home. She slid the last book into its place on the bookshelf, and slowly rose to her feet with a yawn. Every muscle in her body ached, but everything was back in its place. She'd even opened the UPS box and arranged the brightly colored parcels from her parents under the tree. She'd hoped it would help lift her spirits, but it only made her miss them more, and emphasized how alone she would be this Christmas.

At least they had made plans to FaceTime in the morning. It wasn't quite as good as in person, but at least it was something. Nicole yawned again and stretched. She was exhausted. What a long day. She went over to her stereo and flicked off the Christmas music, intending to head for bed, when she suddenly realized she hadn't checked on Missy properly earlier. She'd completely forgotten in the chaos of the afternoon.

Mentally rebuking herself, she shrugged into her heavy

parka and headed out towards the barn. An icy wind whipped across the ground, slicing through her coat, and stinging her cheeks. As she hurried across the yard, she noticed the lights still blazing from Corrie's kitchen window. Garrett's SUV and Dawson's truck were both still parked in front of the house. The family reunion was going well then. Good thing she'd made plans to be elsewhere tomorrow.

Nicole let herself into the barn, and turned on the light. It wasn't terribly bright, but it lit the room adequately. The warm smells of hay and manure greeted her. The cow huffed out a steamy breath in the cold air, while chewing her cud.

Suddenly Missy let out a loud moan. Nicole raced to her stall and looked over the rail. Missy was turning in circles, pawing at the straw-covered ground. She lay down, moaned, stood up, circled and pawed some more. Nicole saw the copious mucous and red staining on her back end. It had started! Missy was in labor.

Oh my gosh! A thrill of excitement coursed through her. Where was her emergency prep kit? Back in the house.

Nicole rushed back outside to get her kit from where it was stored in the mudroom, just in case. It wasn't long before she was back in the barn, watching over her poor goat from inside her stall. Missy let out a long loud 'baa' and arched her back. Her tail arched up and down with the long contraction.

"Poor girl." Nicole stroked Missy's head. She checked her watch and settled in to wait. Considering she didn't know when Missy started contractions, there should be a kid born in less than an hour.

As the minutes ticked by, Missy continued her restless behavior. She was up and down, pawing and circling. She moaned in pain, contracting often, but nothing seemed to happen. As time passed, Nicole became more and more anxious. She paced along with her goat, offering gentle words of encouragement.

She had studied, and read, and watched videos. There should be feet showing by now. Missy was looking exhausted. Nicole had been watching for almost an hour, and there was no telling how long Missy had been in labor before she arrived.

It seemed to last forever. Missy screamed and pushed. Finally, Nicole could see something. She approached Missy's rear, but her gut clenched at what she saw. There was something there, but it wasn't feet. It should be two feet coming first. The kid should arrive, two front feet, head, and a belly flop out. This was wrong. Very wrong!

She needed help. But Garrett was up there still. She didn't want to see him. She didn't want to bother their family, but it was ten thirty Christmas Eve night. Even if she could get ahold of a vet at this hour, would he arrive in time?

Missy bellowed again, and Nicole made her choice. She bolted for the big house.

The two vehicles were still parked in front, and the kitchen light still on as Nicole approached. She raced to the door and pounded on it. The door opened almost immediately, revealing a beautiful brunette with long wavy hair and golden-brown eyes. This must be Garrett's sister, Jess.

"Hello?" Jess said, clearly surprised at the late-night guest.

"Hi," Nicole gasped, trying to catch her breath. "I'm sorry

it's so late. I'm Nicole, the tenant. Is Corrie here? My goat's in trouble. I need help, fast."

"Mom! It's for you," Jess called out, opening the door to admit Nicole into the kitchen. Corrie sat at the table with Dawson on her one side, and Garrett on her other. All three nursed cups of something steamy that smelled of cinnamon.

"What's up, Hon?" Corrie asked, her face concerned.

"Missy's in labor, but something's wrong. She's in trouble. The feet aren't coming out like they should. I need help. Can you come, Corrie?" Nicole begged.

Beside Corrie, Nicole saw Garrett watching her intently. She turned her eyes away. His betrayal still hurt too much. Hands clenched, she turned back towards Corrie.

"I wish I could help, Hon, but landing on my backside earlier today has stiffened my back right up. Garrett can help, though," Corrie suggested.

Garrett. Alone in the barn with Garrett, the love of her life and breaker of her heart. Nicole hesitated. She needed the help, but Garrett? She met his gaze, and found him hesitating, too. So apparently, he didn't want to help any more than she wanted him to.

"I can help," Dawson said, starting to stand to his feet.

Corrie's hand flashed out and caught Dawson's arm, stopping him halfway up. "Didn't you just say you have to leave because you have to get up early tomorrow to feed cattle before coming over? Garrett can help. He'll know what to do."

"I don't mind…" Dawson started to say before stopping abruptly at Corrie's expression.

"Garrett can help," Corrie insisted.

Dawson slid back down in his seat with a shrug. "It's all yours, Super-G."

"Can't you do it, Corrie?" Nicole pleaded.

"If there's any pulling to do, I won't be able to get down there to feel around or pull. Garrett's a doctor. He can help you."

"I'll get my coat," Garrett said, finally rising to his feet. "Do you have towels and lubricant?"

"Yes. My emergency kit is ready."

Her kit was ready, but her heart wasn't. But what choice did she have? Missy needed help fast. A minute later they were hurrying through the yard, back towards the barn.

Nicole heard Missy scream as they opened the barn door. They hurried to the stall to find her lying on her side and straining through another contraction.

Garrett slipped off his coat and shoved up his sleeves. "Disinfectant?"

"Here." She squirted disinfectant lube over his outstretched hands.

"Towel," he said, holding his hand out to receive the towel from her.

Kneeling behind the goat, he wiped the discharge away, and gently slipped his hand in to feel around. He quickly withdrew his hand and stood up.

"It's not good," he announced. "The kid is coming nose first instead of feet first. Its shoulders are stuck."

"What do we do? Can you help her? Should I call the vet?"

"It may take too long to get the vet out at this hour.

Besides, our regular guy is a cattle and horse vet. He isn't familiar with goats. But there's something we can try."

"Anything! Just help her."

"We'll have to try to push the head back in, snag the feet, and try to pull them forward," Garrett explained.

"Do it. How can I help?" She was ready to try anything to help her poor goat.

"That's the catch. I can't do this. My arm's too big. You're going to have to do it."

"Me?" Nicole squeaked. "I've never done anything like this before. I don't know how!"

"You can do this," Garrett encouraged. "I know you can. I'll talk you through it."

*a*s she stared into his eyes, his hands firmly on her shoulders, her courage grew. She could do it. She had to. "Okay. Let's get started."

Minutes later, slim arm lubed up to the elbow with slimy disinfectant, Nicole was positioned behind Missy while Garrett steadied the goat's head and shoulders.

"Reach in, wait 'til the contraction stops, and feel for the nose."

"Got it!" Nicole felt a small, rounded bump that had to be a nose.

"Now push the nose back up the birth canal. Stop and wait if she contracts. Push firmly, slowly."

"Okay. Okay. Got it." Nicole felt a small thrill of triumph. So far, so good.

"Feel around for feet. Slide your hand from the nose, up the neck, and down until you find the shoulder, then follow that down the front leg to the hoof."

Sure. Easy-peasy. Nicole fumbled around blindly trying to follow his instructions. "Ooo! I think I found the leg."

"Good. You're doing great. Now grab the hoof and pull it forward," Garrett coached.

Nicole had to pause for a long, agonizing contraction that had her hand feel like it was in a vise. When it finally passed, she pulled the leg forward. "Got it."

"Good job. Now do the other side."

After some struggle and groping around, Nicole managed to coax the other front leg forward as well. "That's both of them." She grinned up at Garrett who was still holding firmly onto Missy.

"Good! Now make sure the nose is still between the two front legs. The kid should be in a divers position." Garrett grunted as Missy lurched to her feet in spite of his efforts.

"No. The head's off to the side now," Nicole said.

"Pull it forward."

It's too slippery. I can't get a grip." She tried again but her fingers slipped off.

"Find the nose again," Garrett instructed. "Put your finger inside its mouth and grip the lower jaw."

"I got it. I got it!" Nicole exclaimed. She pulled firmly and the little head slid into position. She'd done it, thanks to Garrett.

"Good job! Now slide out."

Nicole withdrew her arm and used one of the clean towels to wipe herself off. She put her coat back on as Missy contracted again. Two front feet appeared.

Nicole stood back and clutched Garrett's arm, laughing. "Look! Feet!"

Two more big pushes and a dark, wet kid belly flopped into the straw.

"Here." Garrett thrust the towel at her. "Wipe off the nose and face so it can breathe."

Nicole vigorously rubbed the baby's face, then its back. It let out a wail, the best sound Nicole had ever heard. She grinned up at Garrett who stood by, watching like a proud papa.

"Put it in front of Missy so she can lick it off," Garrett instructed.

Nicole did, then stood back beside Garrett as Missy began tending to her baby. The tender scene overwhelmed her, causing a rush of relief and gratitude. On impulse she flung her arms around Garrett; hugging him fiercely she exclaimed, "Thank you, thank you, thank you! You saved them!"

Garrett hugged her back, tightly, pressing her deep into his chest, his cheek resting on the top of her head. It reminded her of that kiss, at the party, and stirred to life all those same feelings. Then she remembered things had changed, and it felt like a gut punch all over again. She stiffened in his arms, cleared her throat, and pulled away.

The look of sorrow on his face almost undid her, so she turned away and focused on the goat instead.

"What's that red thing coming out?" It was gross, whatever it was.

"That's the placenta," Garrett answered, his voice cool and detached.

"So she's all done then?"

"Maybe. Let me check." Garrett stepped up to Missy. Putting a hand on either side of her tummy, he bounced it gently up and down a couple of times. "I think there's at least one more kid in there," he concluded.

"Really? Will it need help, too?"

"We'll wait and see." He leaned back against the wall of the stall with his arms crossed in front of him.

Nicole stood back and watched Missy lick her baby off. The little one was already trying to stand on wobbly legs. In the small box-stall, there wasn't much room between her and Garrett. The tension between them was almost unbearable. Even though he wasn't touching her, she could feel the energy arching between them.

She wanted nothing more than to slip her arms through his unzipped jacket, slide them up his back and around his chest, and bury her face into his sweater. She wanted to hear the rhythm of his heart and breathe in the scent of him. Instead, she kept her hands shoved deep in her pockets. No telling where they'd want to roam if given a chance.

She couldn't afford to indulge impossible fantasies, so she held back her traitorous heart. He'd betrayed her trust, just like Tim had. She couldn't allow herself to forget that.

Beside her, Garrett kept taking a deep breath, as if he were about to say something, but then he'd let it go in a sigh, without speaking. She wondered what he wanted to say. Would it even matter? The silence stretched between them, broken only by the rustling of the animals in the straw.

"Mind if I turn on the radio?" Nicole asked abruptly.

"Go ahead," Garrett answered, sounding as relieved as she felt for the distraction.

She left the stall and crossed the aisle to the old radio. She flicked it on to the local station which was playing Christmas music. She strolled back to the stall where Missy was beginning to fuss again.

She resumed her place beside Garrett, so close, yet so far away. She longed for the closeness they'd once shared, but it just wasn't meant to be. Still, she did owe him thanks for earlier in the day.

"I never thanked you properly for today," she offered. "So… Thank you. For coming to my rescue today."

"It was nothing. Norbert did all the heavy hitting." Garrett shrugged off her thanks.

"Still. You were there. You came back. I don't know how you knew we were in trouble."

Garrett shrugged again. "It was just a feeling."

"But you listened this time," she noted.

"I guess I did. I needed to come apologize anyway."

"Oh?" That was interesting. She hadn't expected that.

"Yeah. I finally talked to my parents about the accident and Dad's hand."

"Oh? And how'd that go?" *Sure. Apologize to them, but not to me. Because who cares about dumb old Nicole, right?* Not exactly what she'd hoped.

"Better than I thought, actually. Turns out I was the only one blaming me for it. They forgave me right away."

"That's nice." *Nice for you. You still screwed me over.* She kept her hands stuffed in her pockets, refusing to meet his gaze. The silence stretched between them.

"I, uh, I apologized about the whole realtor thing, too," he said finally.

"Go on."

After a long pause he said, "Nicole, I'm sorry. I guess I

was so determined to make amends for my mistake that I bulldozed over everyone, including you."

"Yes, you did." Nicole turned on him. "After all I told you. How could you?"

"Hang on a second. I made that realtor appointment *before* you told me what had happened in Calgary. I tried to cancel it, but the guy had already left his office and didn't get the message," Garrett explained.

"Regardless," Nicole snapped. "You knew I loved it here, and you didn't care!" She spun her back to him, arms folded across her chest. *I love you and you didn't care.*

"Nic. That's not true." He tried to turn her back towards him, but she shrugged his hand off.

"Nic… I did care. I mean I do care.

"It's just that I thought this place was too much for my parents to handle, even with your help. I figured there were lots of other places you could rent if you really wanted to stay in the country…"

"But I like it *here*," she interrupted.

"Yes. I see that now. But I was hoping…I thought you might only be staying out of obligation to look after them… but if they moved, you'd be free to…you might want to move back…I mean if we lived closer…"

"What *are* you trying to say?" Nicole huffed, turning to face him with hands on her hips.

Garrett sighed, looking miserable. "I wanted you to move back to Calgary."

"Why? Do you hate me so much you can't even stand to let me live here?" The ache in her chest was unbearable. She folded her arms, hugging herself tightly, as her vision blurred.

"No!" He put his hands on her arms, looking deep into her eyes. "It's not that at all. The opposite. I wanted you in Calgary, so you'd be closer to me. Because... Because I love you, Nicole."

She couldn't believe her ears. "What?"

"I love you, Nic. So much. I didn't want to go back to Calgary without you. I'm sorry I hurt you. I never meant to. Please forgive me."

Nicole stared, incredulous. Could it be true? What she'd longed for, what she'd dreamed of? She searched his face.

She could see it then, shining in his eyes. Love. Devotion. Remorse. Warmth bloomed in her chest. Hope swelled, expanded, until it filled her soul. She allowed all the feeling she'd suppressed, all the love in her heart, to surge to the surface and break free. She smiled so wide it almost hurt her face.

Laughing with pure joy she moved forward to hold him, but suddenly, he took a step back, a look of determination on his face.

"There's one more thing," he said, holding her back.

CHAPTER TWENTY-SEVEN

"Go on," Nicole said. The glow on her face dimmed.

He had to tell her, even if she couldn't forgive him for it, even if it ended everything. He owed her that.

"I gave Tim your address. It's my fault he found you," he rushed on. "I am so sorry. I didn't know who he was. It happened at the Christmas party, before I knew your story. See, I bought two of your paintings, and he offered to deliver them, and it just never occurred to me that he wasn't a good guy..."

Nicole just stared at him, silent. He could see she was thinking. *It's over. She hates me.* He straightened his spine. He just had to take it like a man. He braced for her anger.

"You bought two of my paintings?" she asked, a smile tugging the corners of her mouth.

"Well, yeah. They're amazing." *Did you hear me? I almost got you killed.*

"Two?" She stepped closer, her perfume tantalizing. He

swallowed hard. Her eyes pinned him in place, making it hard to think straight.

"Did you hear me, Nic? I'm the reason Tim found you. It's my fault." Why was she grinning?

"I heard you fine. Did you really mean what you said?" She slipped her arms under his jacket, her hands running up his back, sending his pulse racing. She gazed up into his face, her expression thoughtful. She didn't look angry. Why wasn't she angry?

"Yes, I mean it. I am so sorry."

"Not that bit." She shook her head, and murmured, low and throaty, "The other bit."

"Other bit?" He was so confused now.

"You know. The part where you said you love me?" She gazed up at him, her eyes glowing.

It was hard to breathe, his heart hammered so hard in his chest. "Yeah... You're all I can think about. I've been miserable these last few days... but I'll understand if you can't forgive me..."

"I love you, too!" she declared, her smile blinding.

All he could do was stare at her beautiful face, her piercing gray eyes dancing with laughter. Could it be true? "You mean it? You don't hate me?"

"I could never hate you," she purred.

"But I ruined your safe place. You'll be afraid to stay here now."

"Isn't that what you wanted?" Her eyes twinkled with mischief.

"Never. I wanted you closer to me. I never wanted you to be afraid, ever." He met her eyes, willing her to believe him, desperate to make things right.

"Well, relax then, because I'm not afraid anymore." She smiled like the cat who ate the cream.

"No? How's that?" He pulled her closer, resting his cheek on her head. Her hair smelled of strawberry shampoo; her hands around his waist had his senses on fire.

"I guess I finally figured out that it's not a place that makes you safe, it's the people around you. People like your mom...and you."

"Last time was terrifying because I was alone. Tim left me fearful for a long time. But this time, I wasn't alone. You were all there to help, and I overcame because of it. I'm a victor, not a victim. And I'm not afraid anymore. Does that make any sense?" She pulled back to look him in the eye again.

"Yeah. It kinda does." He lowered his face to hers, and kissed her long and slow, showing her all the love he felt in his heart for his beautiful, crazy, goat-loving girl. She melted into him, feeling like she'd been sculpted specifically for him, to be his match in every way. His girl. His world.

Missy let out another loud bleat, startling Nicole. Garrett released her reluctantly.

She bent to see her goat and exclaimed, "There's another one! Garrett, hand me the towel again."

He did, watching her with amused patience as she fussed over the second kid, toweling it off and placing it in front of Missy for her to finish the job and bond to her baby.

"I think it's a girl," Nicole said, grinning up at him from her crouch on the floor. "What do you think?"

Garrett bent to examine the little kid. "Yes. Looks like a girl to me, too. And this other one is a girl as well," he remarked, after checking the first kid to be born. He checked his watch. "Time of arrival, Twelve thirty-five, Christmas morning. What are you going to name them?"

"I dunno. How about...how about...Holly and Ivy?"

"That's definitely Christmassy."

She laughed, music to his ears, and stood to embrace him once more. He pulled her tight to his chest.

"I do love you," he assured her, afraid somehow she still had doubts.

"I love you, too. With all my heart," she answered back, pulling his face down to meet her own.

CHAPTER TWENTY-EIGHT

A year later, Nicole sat on Corrie's big couch, Garrett's arm draped possessively across her shoulders. She snuggled next to him, savoring his warmth, the scent of his aftershave, and the peaceful happiness his presence brought her. All was perfection this Christmas morning now that he was back from Calgary.

On the wall behind them, Nicole's beautiful painting of deer in a fresh-cut field hung on the wall. It still filled her with joy that he'd considered it a suitable gift for his parents last year. A Christmas candle flickered merrily on the coffee table, infusing the air with the scent of cranberry and cinnamon. Crumples of gift wrap and ribbon were strewn across the floor, and lively chatter filled the room.

The rest of Garrett's family gathered around the big Christmas tree in the Pines' living room. Across from them Abram sat on the love seat with Corrie snuggled up beside him. Dawson reclined in the easy chair, his long legs a tripping hazard as they extended out in front of him. Jess, a green felt hat perched on her head, was acting as elf again this year, fetching presents from under the tree and handing them out.

Jess handed Dawson a large box. "From Garrett," she said, perching on the other end of the couch from Nicole to watch him open it.

Dawson ripped the wrapping paper off with ease, only to find the box wrapped like a mummy in layers of clear tape. Garrett chuckled. Dawson gave him a look, slipped a pocketknife from the front of his jeans, and sliced easily through the tape.

"Hey. That's cheating," Garrett complained with a grin.

"That's not cheating. That's just being smarter than my bro'," Dawson laughed. "But, nice try, G-man." Opening the box, he pulled out a new pair of cowboy boots. "Hey! Nice. Thanks, man." He shoved one sock-clad foot in. "Perfect fit."

"Yeah. I figured we were still the same size. You're welcome," Garrett answered.

Dawson leaned back, hands behind his head, legs extended with the new boots on, grinning ear to ear.

"Careful, Daw. I'm going to trip over those bloody long legs of yours," Jess complained. She had to step over him to pull another gift from under the tree and hand it over to her father. "From Dawson."

Corrie steadied the box while Abram pulled the paper off with his one good hand. It opened easily to reveal a beautiful heavy wool sweater with a Nordic pattern in navy, red and white.

"Thank you, Daw," he said, almost perfectly clear. Nicole

smiled to herself. Abram had improved so much in the past year.

"There's only two left," Jess announced. "Mom, this is for you from Nicole and Garrett."

Corrie began the painstaking process of opening her gift without tearing the paper. Nicole couldn't help but laugh to herself at the impatient look on Jess' face.

"Just rip it!" Jess encouraged.

"No. The paper is so pretty…" Corrie finally peeled the paper off. "A new phone! Thank you, guys. The old one hasn't worked right since it got thrown across the yard last year."

"I can't believe it's been a whole year since Norbert broke that guy's leg, and I missed the whole thing," Jess complained.

"Ooo! Don't remind me." Corrie shuddered. "Just thinking about it gives me the shivers. I'm glad I didn't see it happen."

"I can believe it. So much has changed for Nicole and me since then," Garrett remarked.

"That's for sure," Dawson added. "You two are so cute it's nauseating." He ducked, laughing, as Garrett pitched a pillow at his head.

"There's more to it than that," Nicole reminded them. "I started my new position at Red Deer College last September, and the two Christmas kids, Holly and Ivy, are a year old now. I just put them in with Norbert, so we'll have more new babies by May." She looked over at Garrett sitting beside her. He met her gaze with a sultry look that warmed her to her toes. She never would have guessed how great things would work out between them when she'd first moved in. The only thorn in her side was how far away he lived. It was an almost two-hour drive in good weather.

"Well, I have a bit of good news, too," Garrett announced. "I've decided to move my practice out to Red Deer. There's a clinic that's asked me to join them, and I said yes."

"Garrett! You never said a word! This is fantastic," Nicole exclaimed.

"I'm glad you like the idea. I was getting tired of all those long drives back and forth from here to there. This way I can be closer to Mom and Dad, as well as you." His smile warmed her to her core.

"Took you long enough," Dawson said.

"So whatever happened to that guy Norby took out?" Jess asked.

"Oh, Honey. I told you all about that, remember?" Corrie said.

"No, you didn't, Mom. You *think* about telling me stuff, then you forget you didn't actually tell me. You do this all the time. I never get all the juicy news when I'm away at school."

"Remember the key that guy, Tim, was yelling about?" Nicole said. "When the police showed him they had it, he lost all hope and spilled his guts. He told them where the stuff was hidden in a storage unit, and they were able to get a search warrant for it. They found stolen jewelry, cash, and drugs. Tim wound up pleading guilty and rolling on his partner to get a lighter sentence, but he's still going to be locked up for a couple of years at the least."

"Aren't you afraid he'll come back to get revenge?" Jess asked, a hint of fear in her voice.

"No." Nicole shook her head. "After the mess Norbert made of his leg, I doubt he'll ever go near a farm again. I heard he wound up with a metal rod through his femur and several screws to hold it together."

"Ouch!" Jess winced.

"Serves him right," Dawson said, still stretched out in the chair. "Any dummy knows you don't hit a goat on the head unless you want to start a fight." He shook his head in disgust.

"I think there's one last gift, isn't there?" Garrett prompted, shifting in his seat.

Nicole scrutinized him. He looked awfully nervous for some reason.

"Oh, right!" Jess bounced up and retrieved a very small box from the branches of the tree. "Nicole. It's for you."

"Me? Who's it from?" Garrett had already given her several pretty sweaters, and a new jacket, so it couldn't be from him. But who?

She took the small box, and carefully unwrapped the paper. *A jewelry box? What?*

Before she could open it, Garrett reached out and took it from her fingers. "May I?" he said, pulling her to her feet. He then dropped to one knee before her, opened the box with a pop, and revealed the most exquisite pink diamond solitaire.

"Nicole Julianne Mitro, will you marry me?"

Eyes brimming, caught totally by surprise, Nicole could only laugh and nod while holding out her hand for Garrett to slip the ring on. There was a rush of voices and laughter as everyone crowded in to see her joy be made complete.

Outside, Christmas snow fell softly, settling across the backs of Norbert and his harem of does. As the laughter and happy voices drifted out of the house, he stood, gazing across the yard, waiting and watching for the next fool who dared to challenge his supremacy.

Merry Christmas

Thank you for reading *Safe in his arms at Christmas.* If you enjoyed Garrett and Nicole's love story, your honest opinion of their romance matters to this author. Please review this book on your favorite book site, review site, blog, or your own social media properties, and share your opinion with other readers.

A sincere *thank you* for taking the time to write a review!

AFTERWORD

All characters and situations in this novel are fictitious except that Home Church is a real place and 'The Christmas Experience' and 'Christmas is for Everyone' are real events. If you would like to learn more click www.myhomechurch.ca.

CONTACT ELLEN JORGY

You can find Ellen at:
Website: *www.ellenjorgy.com*

Follow Ellen on Social Media

ABOUT ELLEN JORGY

Ellen Jorgy lives in Central Alberta with her husband, Bob, and two children, on a ten acre property with a menagerie of creatures both large and small, including Norbert. After twenty-six years in healthcare she has recently made some changes that will allow more writing, and therefore more joy, in her life.

Her published works include:

An Angel's Secret - A Contemporary Romance set in the mountains of Alberta.

Never Alone - An Inspirational Romantic Suspense.

Safe in his Arms at Christmas - A sweet Christmas-themed Romantic Suspense.

www.ingramcontent.com/pod-product-compliance
Lightning Source LLC
Chambersburg PA
CBHW032155190626
46808CB00020B/425